LUST

Evernight Publishing

www.evernightpublishing.com

SAM CRESCENT

Copyright© 2015

Sam Crescent

Editor: Karyn White

Cover Artist: Sour Cherry Designs

Jacket Design: Jay Aheer

ISBN: 978-1-77233-507-1

ALL RIGHTS RESERVED

LUST

DEDICATION

I want to thank Evernight Publishing for being an amazing publisher, and giving the Trojans MC a home. They're a dream to write for.

Also, I want to thank all of my wonderful readers. Without you, none of this could be possible. I hope you love Raoul's story.

LUST

LUST

Trojans MC, 3

Sam Crescent

Copyright © 2015

Chapter One

Raoul watched as the two sluts that visited the club regularly went down on each other. The brothers were watching avidly. Daisy was already naked with his cock covered in latex ready to join in the fun. One of the women was already a member of the club while the other was trying to become one.

Pike and Mary had gotten married and were away on their honeymoon. Duke and Holly were at the ranch house with his son Matthew. The couple was anxiously waiting for the newest member to be born. The club was quiet, basking in the money after another drug run. Duke wasn't doing another run until after the baby was born, and seeing as how he always went, Raoul figured they weren't going to have another trip for some time. What the hell was he supposed to do with the rest of his fucking life?

The bitch who was close to climaxing groaned as Daisy sank his dick right into her greedy little pussy. Raoul had never seen a bitch so wild before, and especially for Daisy's dick. The brother was going to need to go careful there.

"That bitch has got a serious crush for Daisy," Pie said, coming to sit next to him. Pie was one of his best friends, along with most of the brothers. When everyone shunned him after fucking the *then* president's daughter, Holly, Pie hadn't turned his back on him. Raoul deserved all the shit he got. Fucking Holly had been a revelation in itself for him. He had really thought all women were the same, a bunch of useless bitches who were only after one thing, dick.

Turned out he was completely wrong, but then, besides Mary, Raoul had yet to meet another woman worth anything more than a good fuck.

"It's up to Daisy what he wants to do with that." Raoul tipped the beer bottle against his lips while watching the fuck-fest happening. Daisy was ramming his dick inside the cute little fake blonde while also fingering the redhead.

The redhead wasn't natural though, unlike someone he knew. Raoul pushed those thoughts to the back of his mind. It had been well over six months since he'd last thought about her, the young woman he'd saved from being gang raped. He wouldn't be surprised if he heard that she had to go into therapy.

"Do you think he needs any help?" Pie asked.

Staring at the scene, Raoul's dick started to get hard. "I'll help him in a moment."

"Raoul, you go up there and a couple more women are going to flock to you. You fuck all night long, and they love you for it."

No, they loved his dick, not him, which he didn't mind. He didn't have to care for them for the sick shit he loved to do to them.

"Please, Daisy, please, fuck me. Make it burn."

Pie and Raoul burst out laughing. The woman, he couldn't remember her name, was so obvious in her infatuation. He was surprised that Daisy was even touching her at all. Chip and Knuckles came to join them, watching the little show being put on for them.

"I don't know if Daisy is being cruel or really doesn't see it," Knuckles said.

"Don't care. She fucks everything with a dick, so I imagine Daisy doesn't really know or he doesn't give a fuck." Raoul watched as Daisy pulled out of the sopping woman and moved toward the other woman. He had a condom on, but he made the woman lick his covered dick clean before plunging inside her.

The look of pure menace on the one who had a crush was priceless.

"I'm going to go and help her out."

Putting the bottle back on the counter, Raoul started to unbuckle his jeans on the way toward the angry, glaring woman. Tugging a condom out of the top pocket of his jacket, he tore into it, and grabbed the latex.

Gripping the woman's chin, he forced her to look at him.

"Daisy hasn't claimed you to be his. You better wipe that look off your face or you're out."

This woman hadn't been initiated into the group whereas Samantha, the club whore Daisy was currently fucking, had.

"What's your name?" Raoul asked.

"Lori."

"Well, Lori, it's time for you to put that mouth to good use." Pulling his dick out of his pants, he slid the latex over his shaft. He pressed the tip to her mouth. "Now, open up."

Slowly, he started to slide his cock deep into her mouth, going as far into her mouth as he could.

"Don't use your teeth."

One of the brothers, Crazy, had been caught by a club whore who liked to use her teeth. The brother had fucked her after she'd bitten into the condom, and nine months later, he had a little girl to show for it. Crazy married the club whore, putting his name to the brat he birthed. The girl's name was Strawberry, and she was a beautiful girl, but the relationship her parents had was toxic.

Lori opened her mouth, and he started to use it as a cunt. Thrusting in and out of her mouth, he turned to look at Daisy, who'd stopped paying her any attention. The brother knew, and this was how he was letting her know.

No man would ever share their real woman with another brother. It was one of their strict rules, and no one was allowed to break that rule. Club whores were shared, passed around by the club. An old lady was taken by one man and one man alone. The only time this rule had changed was with Crazy's woman, Suz. They all knew she'd tricked him into marrying her and had tried to fuck each of them at one time after being married. None of the brothers would go near her. She wasn't worth betraying a brother.

When Daisy didn't make a move to stop Lori from sucking his dick, Raoul wrapped her dyed blonde hair around his fist, pushing her over the pool table. He made sure all the brothers saw her pussy. This was what made her a club whore and never an old lady. None of the men wanted others to see what belonged to them.

None of them had seen Holly or Mary's pussy on display. They'd watched them have sex, but never seen the action itself. The brothers had all been discreet. They'd only seen the treasured jewel that they were now asked to look after, to protect. Raoul took the protection of Holly and Mary very seriously.

Slamming his dick inside Lori, he closed his eyes after releasing a groan. She had a tight pussy. In a couple of weeks several of the brothers would have broken her in making her soft like butter. With his hand still buried in her hair, he rode her pussy hard. The brothers around them cheered, telling them to fuck the bitches, to make both women work for it.

Raoul closed his eyes imagining a woman with beautiful deep red hair and shocking green eyes. He gripped the woman beneath him tighter, knowing it wasn't his Zoe. She wasn't ever going to be found in a place like this. She wouldn't go hunting for him even if he wanted her to, which he didn't. This world wasn't for her. She was in college working hard to become someone more important.

Slapping Lori's ass, Raoul growled as he filled the condom, hating what he'd just done.

Pulling away from her body, he moved out of the way as another brother took over. The fuck-fest had started. Leaving the action, he removed the condom, throwing it into the nearest trashcan. He took the bottle of whiskey from the counter, moving toward the kitchen. No one was inside the room. This place was more the old ladies' domain than the men's. It wasn't sexist; it was just how it was.

Sitting on one of the stools, he drank from the bottle. In the next second he had his cell phone in his hand looking at the woman that was destroying him without even realizing it.

"What's going on?" Daisy asked, walking into the kitchen with his jeans undone.

"You're done already?"

"It's not the pussy I want." Daisy snagged the bottle from him. "When it's not the right pussy, once you've come, there's really no need to stick around."

"Lori's got a thing for you. I'd tread carefully. You don't want to end up like Crazy."

"That son of a bitch *is* crazy. I wouldn't have put up with her shit. I'd have done what Duke did, put a fucking bullet in the bitch's skull." Daisy pressed two fingers to his temple, making a gunshot noise.

Chuckling, Raoul put his cell phone away.

"What's with the girl?" Daisy asked.

He wasn't fast enough putting his cell phone away before Daisy saw the picture.

"Do you remember that girl we saved back in the city?" Raoul snatched the bottle back.

"The redhead about to get gang raped?"

"Yeah."

"What about her?"

Blowing out a breath, Raoul stared at the sticker covering the bottle. "Can't get the bitch out of my head." He pressed a finger to his temple. "She's always there, and I can't get her out of it."

He expected to hear laughter or some snide comment. Glancing over at his brother, he saw Daisy frowning.

"You ever thought of going to see her?"

"I can't do it, man. This life is not for everyone."

"A couple of years ago I didn't think it was the life for Holly or Mary, yet they're married to Duke and Pike. Blows my fucking mind to think of those fuckers settled down."

Yeah, it was laughable. Out of all of the men, Duke and Pike were the most unlikely to settle down.

"What about you? What pussy are you wanting?" Raoul asked.

The shutters came down over Daisy's eyes.

"Fine, you don't want to talk. I can't help you."

Taking the bottle of whiskey, Raoul left his brother alone in the kitchen while he drank himself into oblivion.

****

Running the card along her lips, Zoe stared up at the ceiling. She should be studying while her roommate was out, but she couldn't do it. Staring at the name on the card, she frowned. It wasn't even Raoul's card or for his club, yet he'd given it to her to practice firing the gun.

The lessons were all booked, so she only needed to attend. The gun he'd given her was in the top drawer beside her bed. Every night she brought it out, simply staring at it.

This lack of focus was really starting to affect her studies. Her professors were already pulling her up about her lack of attention in class.

Blowing out a breath, she sat up on the sofa as she heard the key in the door. She had a new roommate, Stacey, who'd been with her since the other one left.

The guy with her was one of the bad boys Zoe steered clear of. She quickly grabbed a pillow, placing it in front of her as they both came in, kissing.

"I had a lot of fun tonight," Stacey said.

"The fun is only just beginning," he said, running a hand down her body.

Zoe couldn't contain her disgusted groan. "I'll just leave and pretend I didn't throw up in my mouth."

She got to her feet, no longer caring she was in her nightclothes.

"Shit, Zoe, I didn't know you were still up."

"I'm pleased you took the time to check." Folding her arms over her breasts, she looked at her roommate. "Goodnight."

"Wait, shit, Zoe, this is Landon. Landon, this is my lovely roommate, Zoe." Stacey made the introductions.

"Great to meet you, Landon." If he was listening closely he'd get the hint that it wasn't so great.

"We're in the same pysch class," he said, making Zoe frown.

"We are?" She'd not noticed him before.

"Wow, a guy could really take offence." He chuckled.

"I'm sure Stacey will keep you well and truly happy." *For the next hour at least.*

She dropped the card, bending down to pick it up.

"For crying out loud, Zoe, call him. What's the worst that can happen?" Stacey asked.

"Who is this guy?" Landon asked, drawing the attention back to him.

"It's no one. I'm sorry I interrupted whatever it was you were going to do." Tucking some hair behind her ear, she walked away, listening to Stacey mutter about her obsession.

Closing the door firmly behind her back, she stared down at the card. What harm would it do to find out where he was? She remembered the leather jacket he wore as clear as the name emblazoned on the back. Biting her lip, she fought with what was right to do and what she should do. She shouldn't go looking for trouble, and that's exactly what a biker like Raoul would be.

Get a grip already. He probably doesn't even remember you.

He had loads of women to satisfy every single one of his needs, good or bad. Sitting on the bed, she stared down at the card.

If you don't get this obsession out of your head, you're going to flunk class, and wish you'd seen what all the fuss was about.

Raoul probably wasn't even that good looking and she'd only thought he was because he'd saved her from being gang raped.

Deciding to stop listening to her head, she grabbed her tablet from the drawer beside the gun.

"I can do this. I can look this guy up online."

She didn't have a clue where he lived, but she remembered the name on the jacket. A motorcycle club like that had to have been in the news.

Rubbing her hands together, she typed in the name of the MC club "Trojans". There were a lot of pages of searches. When she noticed the page with the leather jacket, she pulled up the page. Scrolling through the information she found exactly what she was looking for. The address that happened to be in Vale Valley, the town closest to the city, and one she'd stopped through to eat at the diner. They had the best burgers in the state. She grabbed a piece of paper, scrawling down the address.

When she finished, she closed the tablet so she wasn't tempted to search for more. Staring at the address, she shook her head. "No, I shouldn't go and see him."

Putting the address down, she couldn't bring herself to throw the piece of paper in the trash.

"Damn, I've got to do it. I've got to go and thank him and get this crazy thought out of my head." She slapped her head, hating herself at the same time.

Turning the light out, she stared up at the ceiling wishing with all of her might that she could go back to the way things were before she even met him. She wouldn't have to think about the men who'd lured her outside or the attack afterward. They'd not actually raped her, but it still terrified her.

"Oh, yes, Landon, harder, fuck yes."

Rolling her eyes, she tried not to listen. The walls were so thin it wasn't hard to make out the slapping of the headboard against the wall or the guttural groans coming from the two next door.

When the moans finally subsided and there was silence for several minutes, Zoe climbed out of bed, making her way toward the small kitchen. She opened the fridge to grab some milk.

"You really shouldn't sneak around," Landon said, making her almost drop the milk.

"Jeez, don't just sneak up on people. I swear, it's not fucking funny." She pushed some hair out of her eyes, glaring at him. Putting the milk carton on the side, she grabbed a glass. When she turned back around she glared at Landon, who was drinking out of the carton. "If you wanted some milk I'd have poured you some." She wrinkled her nose when she thought about what Landon had been up to. "I so hope you didn't go down on Stacey."

"I didn't. I don't go down on girls that are easy."

She frowned, glancing over his shoulder to look toward her friend. "I really don't want to know or understand you, do I?"

"I like what I like. Stacey's a good time girl. She knows what she's getting herself into."

Taking the carton from him, she poured herself some milk, taking a sip. "Why are you out here and not in there with her?"

"I heard someone sneaking."

"One, this is my apartment and I can sneak around if I want. Two, I wasn't sneaking. I was being quiet in case you were asleep."

"So you weren't waiting until after we fucked to make a move?" he asked.

Zoe simply stared at him. She was in fact a virgin, but being in college and not knowing about sex were two things that didn't actually go together.

Sipping her milk, she started to think about Raoul again.

"Stacey told me about your little obsession earlier."

"Stacey needs to learn to mind her own damned business." Zoe hated her business being talked about with strangers. She and Landon may share a class together, but she didn't know anything about him.

"The Trojans are a rough crowd. Who are you interested in?" Landon asked.

Frozen in place, Zoe stared at him. "You know them?"

"I know them. I'm not well informed about the whole club. After college I'm hoping to prospect with them."

"You want to be part of the Trojans MC? Can you become a member?"

"Baby, it's not like the mafia where they're born into it. Some members are born into it, and others have to show their worth to become a member."

She didn't think she'd ever meet anyone who'd know of them. All this time she'd been in class with a guy who wanted to be a member.

"I've been to some of their parties. They play hard and fight harder than any bunch of bikers I know."

"You know a lot of them?" she asked, intrigued, excited, and nervous.

"I know them. If you want, this weekend I can take you to them."

Biting her lip, she stared at him uncertain. "I don't know you."

"Honey, I'm not some rapist. If you want to come with me to party then I'm more than happy to take you. I'll warn you. The parties are not conventional. You may be biting off more than you can chew."

She glared at him. "I can handle it. You're on." Placing her open palm between them, she waited for him to shake on it. He grabbed her hand, and pressed a kiss to her knuckles. Snorting, she pulled her hand away, wiping it on her pajama pants.

"You're going to need to be able to handle more than a kiss to be ready for this party."

Sticking her tongue out, she took her glass of milk back to the bedroom. She didn't care what it took. She needed to see Raoul at least one more time.

Chapter Two

Raoul walked toward Drake's house just as he heard a feminine cry. He'd been the one to draw the short straw to take care of Holly while Drake took Matthew down to the lake to fish. With a new baby on the way, Drake didn't want Matthew to feel left out. It was sweet but unnecessary. Matthew was looking forward to a sister or brother.

Entering the house, he didn't immediately sense trouble or danger. Walking through to the kitchen, he frowned when he saw Holly slam a saucepan on the side multiple times before throwing it into the sink.

"You know that could break the sink," he said, leaning against the nearest wall. The sink in question being a large ceramic one, but it looked in one piece. She turned to look at him, shooting him a glare.

"Why are you here?"

"I thought I'd stop by."

She kept staring, and he saw the cogs turning in her head. "My dad on Wednesday, my mother on Thursday, Daisy yesterday, and now you. Duke's put you all on duty to take care of me, hasn't he?"

"He's worried about you."

"No, he's being overprotective. You guys have far more interesting things to do than taking care of me." She folded her arms over her chest.

"You can stare at me all you want. I'm doing exactly what the Prez says."

"And you're all about taking orders?" Sarcasm dripped from her voice.

"Say what you like, Hols. Everyone is looking forward to the brat being born." The entire club was looking forward to it. Duke couldn't stop showing off the ultrasound photos.

"I can't wait for it to be out. Look at me, I'm the size of a tank." She ran her hand over her swollen stomach.

Holly had always been a fuller woman, but she didn't look like the size of a tank. The clothes she wore graced her curves, emphasizing her prominent bump. She looked sexy yet motherly. Being married to Drake suited her.

"You're fine." He sat down at the stool. "Why is it women forget they're carrying another human being? You're not going to stay the same shape with another human inside you."

"Easy for you to say. Men have it bloody easy. They screw us, get an orgasm out of it, and don't have to carry a big lump for nine months. You guys don't have to worry about the morning sickness, sore nipples, feeling horny, or the swollen ankles." She stuck her lip out.

"We suffer with being horny. I'm sure Duke's keeping you well satisfied."

"Keep it up and I'll get Duke to kick your ass."

Raoul chuckled then stopped to look at Holly. "We're good right? You and me?"

"Yeah, we're good. Why?"

"I know shit wasn't normal between us, and I really want to apologize for what I did to you." On her prom night, Raoul had taken her on a date and claimed her virginity. Instead of keeping that piece of information to himself, he'd told the entire club. After he got his ass kicked by Russ, who'd been the Trojans MC president at the time, everything had gone back to normal. Holly had never been the same with him again.

"It's water under the bridge. We slept together. Duke knows about it. There's nothing between us. Besides, I think between my father, the boys at the club, and Duke, you've more than made up for it." She shrugged. "We're good."

He was pleased. "So, why were you beating the shit out of the saucepan?"

She released another growl. "I'm trying to get a caramel to softly set, but the heat just makes it rock hard. I think I'm either not doing enough to start off with or I've got to be patient. I don't know. I'm cursing the big belly. I can't move as fast because I'm waddling like a damn penguin."

It wasn't that bad, but he kept his opinions to himself.

"Is there anything I can do?"

"No." She turned the tap on immersing the pan in water.

"Have you heard from Mary?"

She nodded, smiling. "She's having the time of her life with Pike all to herself. She's loving it. Anything going on at the club?"

"Nothing. We're all waiting for the squirt to drop."

"Duke's already told me he's not going on any more runs. I'm really pleased. If he was away on club business and I went into labor without him, I'd be so pissed." She placed her hand on her stomach. "We want Daddy home, don't we?"

Raoul chuckled. "He's going to be home for a while. He'll not leave your side until he knows you're safe and protected."

Holly's cheeks turned a deep red. She really did glow from the pregnancy.

"While you're here, you may as well put those muscles to good use. Please wash the dishes. I'll make sure there's a great big slice of chocolate cake in it for you."

He didn't need to be told twice. Chocolate cake was his favorite. For the next hour he had his arms in hot water and bubbles to remove the burnt on caramel. This was pure torture. Caramel wasn't designed to come off pans easily. He listened to Holly talk about everything. He discovered Matthew was mostly doing great at school but flunking math. Duke was freaking out when she'd wake in the middle of the night to take a pee. There was a hell of a lot of shit Raoul was finding out that he actually didn't want to know about.

Once he finished with the caramel stuck pan, he finished the rest of the dishes, which earned him a chocolate cake as a reward.

They were both in the sitting room watching an action movie when Duke entered with Matthew not too far behind him.

"How did the fishing go?" Holly asked, getting to her feet. Duke placed a hand on her shoulder, keeping her in her chair.

"Good. It went good."

"If you keep manhandling me, I'm going to hit you where it hurts."

Why did women always get defensive when men were only trying to look out for them?

"Fine, fine, fine," Duke said, raising his hands in surrender.

"I'm heading back to the clubhouse."

"Okay, thanks for keeping her company."

Holly snorted.

"I'm trying to protect you."

"I wouldn't put this baby at risk."

Raoul said his final goodbyes before heading out to his bike. It was cute listening to the couple argue, but he had other things to do. Straddling his bike, he turned over the engine. He didn't allow himself the pleasure of listening to the growl like he usually did. Heading toward the clubhouse, Raoul needed to sink his dick into a nice warm pussy in order to stop himself from going hunting for a woman of his own. In his mind all he saw was the terrified expression of a beautiful, innocent redheaded woman with pretty green eyes filled with fear.

He promised himself he wouldn't see her again. The last trip where he gave her a gun was more for her own protection than his.

Raoul wanted Zoe to be able to protect herself in the future. He couldn't handle the thought of her being helpless.

Entering the compound he already saw the party was in full swing. With Duke spending most of his time with Holly at the ranch and Pike away on his much needed honeymoon, Russ was keeping an eye on things.

The older man was outside, sipping at a beer while checking out the time.

He looked up when he heard the sound of a bike, or at least that's what Raoul believed.

"How's Holly?" Russ asked.

"She's doing great. Annoyed as hell that everyone keep fussing over her but she's got to learn we're not going to let anything happen to her." He climbed off the bike, chaining it in line with the others.

"Sounds like her mother. Sheila wouldn't have anyone around her when she was pregnant either."

"Where is she?" Usually Russ rarely visited the clubhouse during parties without his old lady in tow.

"She didn't feel up to it."

There was a bigger story there that Raoul didn't want to get involved in.

"I'm going to head on in." Entering the clubhouse he saw Daisy was already balls deep in pussy with Pie and Knuckles as his wingmen. The crowd was thriving, practically fucking everywhere.

The moment Daisy saw him, he called for him to join in. "Come on, Raoul, help me get this bitch fucking hot."

From the sight of her, she was already screaming in orgasm. There wasn't much more for him to do.

Raoul kept his jacket on, pulling out a condom from his back pocket. All it took for him to get hard was to imagine a little redhead, and he was good to go.

Pulling his dick out of his pants, he watched Daisy ramming into the girl's pussy, taking what he wanted without caring of the woman beneath him.

"You want my dick, slut?" Raoul asked. She was another regular visitor to the club. He didn't know her name or what she was up to outside of the club. His cock was staying in the latex condom.

****

"Stacey wanted to come for the ride, but I told her no," Landon said, talking. Ever since he'd picked her up from her apartment, he'd been talking.

"Look, I don't care. I only hope Stacey doesn't see us together and think we're a couple. I wouldn't date you."

Landon burst out laughing. "I don't date. I fuck."

"Again, I don't care what you do." Zoe kept to her side of the car. "You know, you're the first guy I know who likes talking. Usually men like silence."

"I guess I'm not like a lot of men."

"You're not actually." She glanced over at him to see he was laughing at her. "You find it funny?"

"No, I find you funny. Stacey told me you were all reserved as hell. No one could get past that frosty exterior. There's a hell of a lot more to you than meets the eye." He shrugged. "You're also the first girl not to fall at my feet."

I'm falling at the feet of another bad boy.

"Don't worry about it. I'm sure the female population on campus more than makes up for my overall lack of caring."

"You've got that right, starting with Stacey."

Zoe didn't want to talk about Stacey. The fact she'd heard her friend have a screaming orgasm over the past week, wasn't something she liked to think about. At least Stacey hadn't called her out in the middle of the night to a club where she almost got gang raped. She really wasn't having the best experience when it came to roommates lately.

"We're almost there," he said.

Her hands started to shake. She didn't know if this was the right thing to do or not. Crap, she really should have spent the last couple of days really thinking about what this would mean when she finally saw him again.

This wasn't a chance meeting. Landon was going to witness everything, and that she didn't want to happen.

Too late.

He pulled up within the clubhouse compound where the party was really getting on. She noticed a much older man outside, smoking a cigarette. He wore a leather jacket, and looked completely at ease.

"That's Russ. He used to run things here," Landon said, turning off the engine of the car.

"Great. He looks … scary as hell."

"Nah, don't get on his bad side. He's not a threat to you, I promise."

Landon opened the door, climbing out of the car. She did the same.

You can do this.

"Hey, Landon. It's been a long time since you've been here, kid."

"I've been busy with school."

"Who's this ripe peach?" Russ asked.

It was strange, but she didn't get the creepy older man vibe from him.

"This is the lovely Zoe." Landon pushed her forward.

What do I do?

"It's nice to meet you," she said, holding her hand out to him.

Russ smiled. "You brought a little sheep into the lions' den."

"Hey, I resent that," she said, before Landon answered.

He raised a brow. She didn't even look behind her to see what Landon was doing. The last thing she wanted to do was think about herself being caught between the two strong men.

"You think you're ready for a club party?"

"I'm more than ready. I told Landon to bring me myself."

"I offered to drive her," Landon said. Glancing over at him, she shot him a glare. "Go ahead and give me the stink eye. It's the truth."

"Take her in. I'm sure an experienced college girl could handle anything."

Not that experienced.

She kept her lips closed.

Landon threw his hand over her shoulders leading her toward the main clubhouse.

"He seemed nice," she said. Landon threw his head back, laughing. "What?"

"Russ is a great guy but don't mistake him being nice for causing shit."

"I'm not going to cause shit."

"Russ used to be the Prez here. He'll kill anyone who tries to fuck with the Trojans."

"Even me?" she asked, looking back at the friendly man.

"You try to fuck with the club, he wouldn't even bat an eyelash at killing you."

She shivered. The thought of anyone committing murder terrified her. Wouldn't it be bad if she didn't shudder?

"What's going on?" she asked.

The whole of the club was looking toward the end of the clubhouse. The sexual moans and groans were easy to detect, but from the look of everyone, they were all about to fuck.

Somehow they were pushed forward with the energy of the club. Landon held onto her arms, keeping her close by his side, or front, as he stood directly behind her.

The moment they broke through the crowd, Zoe froze. There on the dance floor was the very man she'd been obsessed with. He was beside the other one she remembered, Daisy. They were both semi-naked, both wearing their leather jackets while their jeans were around their ankles.

She no longer heard the crowd or what Landon was saying to her. Zoe couldn't tear her gaze away from the man who was fucking one of the women in the ass as he teased another with his fingers.

It was a fuck-fest. Hungry men and women taking pleasure in each other as the crowd cheered for them to fuck and play.

"I tried to warn you," Landon said, whispering against her ear.

"I know." She was breaking apart, and yet the sight before her was … amazing. Being a virgin hadn't been something she was by choice. Every guy she'd been out with had just seemed lacking in every department.

Raoul wouldn't want me.

It was pitiful, stupid, and it was time to get over her silly obsession with him. He had a harem of women at his disposal. She looked around the room and the women eyeing the scene, clearly wanted to be the ones getting fucked.

She turned her gaze back to Raoul, and stopped. He was staring right at her. At first his gaze looked a little hazy, but then he glanced up at Landon, before coming back to her. She recognized the shock, and she didn't need to see anything more.

Tearing out of Landon's grip, she rushed toward the exit. The same door that she entered now beckoned for her to run away. Rushing out the door, she almost charged into Russ.

"Find what you're looking for?" Russ asked.

"More than you'll ever understand." She didn't stay to linger, moving as fast as she could toward Landon's car. Zoe hoped he took the hint that she no longer wished to linger.

"Zoe?"

It wasn't Landon's voice that called her name.

She stood behind the trunk of the car. *Don't turn around. Don't let him see you.*

Again, he spoke her name, and she couldn't exactly ignore him. Spinning around, she gave him her best fake smile

Landon was standing by Russ. The two were talking.

"Look at me, Zoe," Raoul said.

Biting her lip almost to the point of piercing the skin, she stared at the man who'd been in her thoughts for a long time.

"You're looking good," she said, speaking the first thing that came to her mind.

"What are you doing here?"

"I was looking for something, and I think I found it." *Oh, boy did I find it. My fucking sanity. What the hell was I thinking coming to a place like this for a man I don't even fucking know?*

She cursed all the time in her head.

"Is everything okay?" he asked, taking a step toward her.

Taking a step back, Zoe stared at his hands. She knew exactly where they'd been, and she didn't want *those* hands anywhere near her.

"I'm fine. I'm just waiting for Landon to drive me back to campus."

"You don't have to leave."

"I do. I just wanted to see you to thank you. I really didn't mean to interrupt your fun." She moved around the car putting as much distance between them as possible. His jeans were still unbuttoned. He probably still wore the condom. Opening the passenger door, she stared at his shoulder, hoping she was fooling him. "Thank you."

Climbing into the car, she waited for Landon to climb in.

Raoul rounded the car, though, opening the door. "Is anyone giving you trouble?"

She stared into his blue eyes. He had the boy next door look going for him.

"No. No trouble whatsoever." She forced a smile to her lips.

Landon climbed into the passenger side, and she was grateful.

There really were no other words that needed to be spoken between them. Raoul closed the door, and part of her was sad to see him give up so easily. What she'd seen hadn't been that shocking. No, what shocked her was her own reaction to witnessing such open sex. Her body was humming with pleasure. She'd never felt anything like this before, and that alone scared her.

Chapter Three

"I told you to keep an eye on her, not to bring her to the fucking clubhouse and especially not to bring her when I didn't fucking know about it." Raoul yelled at Landon while also pacing the clubhouse parking lot. He was pissed off, more than pissed. Not only had he been close to orgasm last night when he'd happened to glance up and see Zoe, but afterward he'd not been able to do a damn thing. She was too fucking young for him, and there was no chance in hell for either of them getting together.

It was a fantasy inside his own head. He'd seen the shock on her face last night with what she'd witnessed.

You didn't see disgust though.

She had run from him before he witnessed anything else.

"I left a message with Daisy. It's not my fault that he didn't pass it on to you."

"He told me you were coming, not that you were bringing the very woman I put you with to protect." Landon was one of their youngest potential prospects. He was of college age, and he was already in the same college as Zoe. Raoul offered to vote for him to become a prospect, and in return he kept an eye on Zoe.

"I'm there, okay. I'm fucking her roommate."

"Is this the same roommate that almost got her hurt?" Raoul asked.

"No. It's the new one. The old one took the hint when I told her to get out of town." Landon ran fingers through his hair. "Look, I've been talking with Stacey, the roommate, and she told me Zoe is obsessed with you."

"What?"

"She clings to that card you gave her. From what Stacey has told me she hasn't even used the gun you gave her. She's totally focused on you."

Raoul ran a hand down his face. He'd not gotten the best night's sleep last night.

"What's up with you miserable fuckers?" Crazy asked, walking out of the clubhouse. It was one of the first nights he'd actually stayed at the club.

"Where's Strawberry?" Raoul asked, talking about his young kid.

"At home with her mother. I couldn't stay there another minute listening to Suz fucking moan about shit. I tell you, don't ever get fucking married."

"Duke's married. So is Pike," Landon said.

"They're lucky bastards. Holly and Mary are two of a kind. The rest of them are fucking whores." Crazy pulled his cigarettes out of his pocket. "What's going on with you bitches this morning?"

"Raoul's chewing my ass out for bringing his girl here."

"His girl?"

"Zoe, the one he saved a few months back."

"She's not my fucking girl, and it's not any of your fucking business." Raoul glared at each man, hating both of them. "Where is she now?"

"I took her home. She's probably spending her weekend staring at the card and the gun."

"What else did she say?" Raoul asked.

"Wow, you've really got a thing for this girl, haven't you?" Crazy asked, taking a long draw on his cigarette.

"Fuck off."

"Fine. I'll give you a little piece of advice, don't knock them up."

"You didn't mean to knock Suz up," Raoul reminded him.

"Don't I fucking know it. Suz thinks it's fucking funny that she caught me with the oldest trick in the book. Part of me wished I could be like Prez and shoot the bitch."

They were all killers, but none of them liked killing women. Even Duke had put up with a cheating bitch for a wife before he found Holly. When Julie put Holly's life at risk, Duke cracked, putting a bullet in her head.

Raoul was about to leave the group when Crazy's car pulled into the parking lot. He frowned as Suz climbed out of the car, popping some gum. "I need some money," she said, looking straight at Crazy.

Calling Suz a bitch was insulting the word bitch. There was no one she cared about but herself. Out of all the women Raoul knew, she was the least maternal, even less so than Julie.

"Where's fucking Strawberry?" Crazy asked.

"How the fuck should I know?"

Anger emanated out of Crazy. He was positively throbbing with rage. "Where's my daughter? I mean it, Suz."

"I don't know. It was your night last night. I've not seen her. Now, I want my money."

"Last night was your night to spend with her. I left her with a babysitter." Crazy threw his cigarette to the floor.

"Oops, I guess I forgot. Oh well, money." She held her palm out.

Raoul was sick to his stomach to witness the woman's complete lack of care.

Crazy walked up to her, but he didn't go into his pocket. He grabbed Suz around the neck, pressing her against the car. Raoul didn't make a move toward him. The bitch deserved whatever Crazy decided to give.

"Shouldn't you stop that?"

"He's just realized his little girl may have been left alone all last night. Wouldn't you be pissed if it was your kid?"

Crazy talked quietly, whispering the words against her ear. From the fear flashing across her face Crazy wasn't holding back in his threats.

Finally, he gave her some money. When she went to argue he shot her another warning.

He moved back toward them as her car rushed out of the parking lot. "I've got to head home."

"Is Strawberry on her own?"

"No. I left her with the babysitter. I'll just have to pay her extra for the time she's been taking care of her."

"Who's your babysitter?" Landon asked.

"The woman who lives across the hall from me, Leanna." Crazy stretched. "I'll see you guys around."

"I want you to take Stacey out this afternoon," Raoul said, giving the order to Landon when they were alone.

Landon groaned. "Man, do you know how clingy this bitch is?"

"You should have made sure I got the message yesterday. I don't really give a fuck how needy this girl is. Take her out, fuck her, dine her, whatever. I don't care." Raoul left him alone, heading back inside. Daisy was sitting at the bar, nursing another coffee. "We're always doing this."

"Fuck, man, don't speak so loud. Anyone could hear you." Daisy rubbed at his temples.

"What's going on with you?"

"I party hard and fuck hard. I'm not as young as I used to be." Daisy groaned. "Fuck, I think I'm going to be sick."

Daisy rushed out of the room, heading toward the nearest bathroom.

"Hey, Raoul," Lori said.

Lori was walking up behind him. When she made to touch him, he grabbed her hands, stopping her from doing it. "Don't even think about it."

"Why? You liked what I was doing to you last night." She tried to whisper against his ear. Gripping her neck, much like Crazy had with his woman, Raoul applied pressure to her throat.

"I suggest you get the fuck away from me before I end your poor excuse for a miserable life. You're good enough for a fuck, Lori. Nothing else. Get out of here."

She ran away, grabbing her bag from the pile and leaving the clubhouse. Minutes later Daisy came back, looking around the corner. "Is she gone?"

"Was that all a fucking act?" Raoul asked.

"Not all of it. My head is fucking killing me. That woman is like a leech, and I can't get her off me." Daisy took a seat at the bar, looking a little more human than he had a few moments ago.

"What's with the faking?"

"I can't stand her. She's good to take my dick, but I don't want her. That woman is trying to become an old lady."

"You think she's trying to do to you what Suz did to Crazy?"

"I'm not falling for it. I won't let her near me." Daisy took a sip of his coffee. "What are you doing today?"

"I'm going to head out. I've got to see someone." He didn't want to tell him that he intended to see Zoe.

"I take it you don't need a brother to come along for the ride."

"Not for this one." Rubbing the back of his head, Raoul stretched, checking the time. He didn't want to go too early. When he saw Zoe he wanted to be alone. From what Landon had told him, Stacey wasn't the kind of girl he wanted around Zoe.

After an hour of hanging around the club, he climbed on his bike, and headed toward the apartment.

For the first time in his life, Raoul was nervous. He didn't know what it was about Zoe, but she'd gotten under his skin and now he couldn't just get rid of her.

Blowing out a breath, he made his way toward her building.

****

Zoe blew over the rim of her coffee and tried not to think about last night. When she'd finally fallen asleep, she'd had dreams of Raoul, only it wasn't the woman he'd been with. No, in her dream, it had been her that had been in place with Raoul's cock tunneling inside her.

She'd woken up in a sweat and filled with need that had taken her breath away.

Stacey was already gone for the day. Landon had picked her up, and Zoe and Landon both acted oblivious to the other. She didn't want Landon to look at her. Last night *had* happened. She only wished he'd not witnessed her stupidity.

The card that Raoul had given her was on the counter in front of her, mocking her. She'd been having dreams about a fantasy.

Raoul wasn't the kind of man she wanted to be with. Yet he was the first man who'd ever inspired any kind of response inside her.

Someone knocked on her front door, and she wondered if Stacey had forgotten her keys. Climbing down off the stool, she made her way toward the door, opening it with a smile that soon died on her lips.

"Hello, Zoe," Raoul said.

"Hello, Raoul." She simply stared at him, shocked that he was on her doorstep. "What are you doing here?"

"You should have known I'd come to you after last night." He leaned against her doorframe, and she wasn't even tempted to slam the door in his face.

"Why?"

"I left you with instructions to take lessons with the gun I'd given you. Have you done it?"

"No."

"Why?"

"I don't want to learn how to shoot a gun." Turning on her heel, she left the door open, giving him the chance to walk into her apartment. Part of her wanted him to stay outside, but she couldn't stand in front of him while trying to talk.

The sound of the door closing along with his footsteps made it all final to her.

"You need to learn how to shoot for your own protection."

"This isn't the wild west. I'm not some woman in a saloon, Raoul. I don't need to know how to use a gun to survive. I can survive all on my own and with Mace spray." She folded her arms underneath her breasts, facing him.

The moment she stared into his eyes, she found it impossible to think.

"Why did you come to the clubhouse last night?"

"I wanted to see you." She figured going with the truth would make him leave her alone a little faster.

"Why?"

"Will you stop asking that?"

"No."

"Well, I'm not going to tell you why I wanted to see you." It was embarrassing. While she'd been thinking constantly about him, he'd been screwing every woman he could get his hands on.

"You don't need to hide anything from me. What you saw—"

"What I saw put a lot of things into focus for me."

"You can't stop thinking about me." He didn't make it sound like a question. "I spoke to Landon," he said, when she frowned at him.

"Is that why he's taken Stacey out? Did he know you were coming here?" she asked. She'd not even thought about Landon knowing Raoul.

Stupid, stupid, stupid, he spoke with that guy last night like he knew him.

This entire trip was getting a little too weird for her.

"Yes. He's here because I asked him."

"What do you mean?"

"I asked him to keep an eye on you."

"I don't need a babysitter." Why did he have someone looking after her? She was so angry with him right now. It wasn't fair to Landon that Raoul was making a guy like Landon look after her. Yes, she'd been in danger, but that was the first time she'd ever been in trouble.

"Let's not argue about this."

"There's nothing to argue with. I made a mistake. Tell Landon to back off." She glared right back at him.

"You wanted something from me. What was it?" he asked, taking a step toward her.

She forced herself to stay still. It would be all too easy for her to step back and ignore him.

"I don't want anything from you."

"Don't lie to me, Zoe. You've been thinking about me."

Zoe sealed her lips, refusing to give him the satisfaction. "You've got more than enough women to warm your bed."

"I don't want women to warm my bed, Zoe. They were keeping my dick wet, nothing else."

"Will you please leave?" She wasn't used to feeling jealous, and the way he was talking was making her jealous. Zoe didn't want to think about the other women he'd been with.

"No." He closed the small distance between them. Zoe tried to take a step back, but he wouldn't let her. Raoul grabbed her arms, tugging her close. Her arms touched his leather jacket. The heat from his hands wasn't helping her ability to think. Gritting her teeth, she forced herself to stare at the patch on his leather jacket.

There's nothing special about him.

He's a biker.

He's nothing to me.

It was all lies, but she'd do anything to rid herself of any kind of good memory of him. He'd been the first and only man to really help her. That night those months back could have gone a whole lot worse without his help.

"I'm not going to leave until you tell me why you came to see me."

"I just wanted to say thank you. I've said it, and now I don't need to say it anymore. You can keep Landon away." She tried to move away from him. Raoul wouldn't let her. His thumbs stroked over her arms

Against her better judgment, she stared down at his lips. Taking a deep breath, she couldn't believe what was happening to her body. The fire began to build within her. She pressed her thighs together at the slick heat coming from her pussy. Her nipples grew hard at his closeness.

He was with another woman just hours ago.

Raoul leaned forward, and his lips touched her ear. "Tell me to go, Zoe. Tell me to go right now."

She opened her lips to tell him exactly that. Only she stopped. Biting her lip, she couldn't bring herself to tell him to stop or to leave.

I want him.

"I mean it, Zoe. There's only so much I can take. This is your last chance."

Say it.

Don't say it.

What will he do if I don't say it?

Keeping her lips closed, Zoe tilted her head to the side, and stared up at him.

"Big fucking mistake." The hands on her arms slid up going into her hair. She gasped, and in the next second his mouth was devouring her lips. He held her close, his fingers gripping her hair as he sucked her bottom lip into his mouth, biting down.

She unfolded her arms, gripping his shoulders tightly.

One of his hands left her hair, gliding down her back to go to her ass. He squeezed her ass tightly, drawing her close to him. The moment she touched him, she felt the hard ridge of his cock pressing against her stomach.

An image of his cock sinking into another woman invaded her senses.

"No," she said, pulling away from him, long enough to get her sanity back.

"What is it?" he asked, kissing her head.

"What about last night? I don't want to step on anyone's toes."

"The women last night didn't mean a fucking thing to me. I use them, Zoe. I've been using them ever since I first met you. You've been in here." He pressed a finger to his head to show her exactly where she'd gotten under his skin. "You're too fucking young."

"I'm not young, Raoul. I want this. I want you."

"You're in college."

"I'm of age. I'm not so young," she said, no longer wanting him to leave. She should be even more pissed off with him being with other women, but she wasn't.

"Are you a virgin?"

"Yes." She frowned at him. "Does it really matter?"

"It should matter."

Taking her hand from his shoulder, she reached out to cup his dick, rubbing him through his jeans. "I don't want you to care who I am." She was tired of only ever wanting, and never getting the chance to experience it.

Listening to Stacey, seeing Raoul with those other women, and after everything that had happened to her, she was tired of always waiting.

She held onto his hand, stepping backward toward her room. Zoe was thankful nothing hindered her walk back to her bedroom. Raoul took over, dragging her into his arms as he led her in the same direction that she'd tried to walk. His palm cupped the back of her head and his other banded around her waist.

"There's no turning back. Once we enter your bedroom, I won't stop."

"I don't want you to stop. I don't expect anything else from you." She needed this. Zoe needed to get the obsession for this man out of her mind. The moment they slept together, it would be over. She'd stop thinking about him and be able to move on with her life.

Deep down she really did believe that to be true.

They stepped over the threshold of her bedroom. This was it. Pushing his leather jacket off his shoulders, she ran her hands down his body, going to the belt holding up his jeans.

She was more than ready for him.

****

Crazy let himself into his apartment. There was no noise, and he reached behind his back for the gun. Silence in his world meant danger. He closed the door quietly and made his way around the apartment, going through the kitchen, then down to the two bedrooms. The apartment was a cheap one. He didn't want to give Suz anything more than she deserved, especially when their daughter was so young. Entering the nursery, he paused as he took in the sight before him.

Leanna, the woman who babysat for him, held Strawberry close to her. His little girl was nuzzled against Leanna's tits, holding her tightly as if she didn't want to let the woman go. Not once had he seen Strawberry do that with Suz. His baby tried to stay as far away from her mother as possible.

He put the gun away. The last thing he wanted to do was scare the woman who'd been nothing but kind to him. Leanna was a darling, beautiful and sweet. He'd checked her out, and she was in her early thirties and had been married once before in her life. She was shy for her age. Crazy found her utterly adorable.

Easing down into the nearest chair, he watched the two as the sun came up. He imagined Strawberry had kept her up until really late. There were six books piled on the floor beside the bed.

The chair he sat on creaked as he moved, waking Leanna up. She placed a hand to her forehead before wiping her eyes.

"What time is it?" she asked.

"It's around ten."

"At night?" She frowned.

"No, it's early morning."

"Ten is not early morning."

"You don't need to rush to get up." He held his hand out so she wasn't afraid.

She stared down at Strawberry. With delicate hands, she started to loosen the girl before easing out of the bed.

Leanna tucked her back in before stretching. "She didn't go to sleep until three." He watched her yawn, pressing a hand against her mouth as she did.

Crazy winced. Even partying he was in bed by then. They walked out of the room, and he was even more surprised as she started to gather everything up, and put it away. Suz refused to clean the apartment, so he hired a cleaner every week to take care of the small apartment.

"I thought Suz was coming back," Leanna said.

"I'm really sorry. She forgot." He winced the moment he said the words.

"Forgot?" He saw how hard it was for her to think about forgetting her kid. If Strawberry was Leanna's, she wouldn't forget about her.

"Yeah, she's a real piece of work."

"I don't feel comfortable talking about this." She grabbed her jacket from the back of the sofa.

"What do I owe you?" Crazy asked, pulling out his wallet.

"Nothing. You don't owe me anything. I love taking care of Strawberry." She looked down the hallway to where his daughter slept. "You've got yourself a little angel there, Crazy. I'm happy to help when you need me."

Not once in his life had a woman refused money from him.

"Thank you," he said, meaning it.

She nodded. "I'm going to see myself out."

He watched her glide past, going to the door. Crazy didn't stop her even as he wanted to. When the door clicked closed, he walked back down to Strawberry's bedroom. She was wide awake, holding the pillow that Leanna had been lying on.

"I like her, Daddy," she said, climbing off the bed. "She bakes cookies."

His heart was breaking. Strawberry loved a woman who wasn't her mother. There wasn't anything he could do at the moment. He doubted there would ever be anything he could do.

Chapter Four

Raoul tugged his shirt up over his head while Zoe started on his belt. Placing his hands over hers, he took them away from the belt.

"There will be time for that." He nudged her back against the bed, tearing her shirt from her body. She wore a white lace bra that showed off the dark red of her nipples. His mouth watered for a taste of her body on his tongue. "Lie back."

Zoe eased down on the bed, and he caught the pants resting on her rounded hips. Sliding the loose pants down her body, he took her lace underwear along with them.

"Open your thighs."

Her cheeks were a lovely red from her blushes, which contrasted with her red hair.

She was already soaking wet.

Raoul sank to his knees before her, pulling her back to the edge of the bed. No other man had touched her pussy. She was untouched, pure, and all his.

Holly had been a virgin, but then he'd not appreciated the sight before him. Zoe was a treasure, a precious jewel within his crazy world.

"What are you doing?" she asked. "Is there something wrong?"

"There's nothing wrong. You just lie back, baby. I've got everything handled here." Placing her feet on his bent thighs, he spread the lips of her sex open, staring at her swollen clit. He took her nub into his mouth, sucking her in deep. Zoe cried out, and he watched her hands grip the blanket beneath her. Sliding his tongue up and down her slit, he groaned at the explosion of flavor. He didn't like going down on a woman as the last thing he ever wanted was to taste another man's cum.

Zoe was pure. The only cum that would fill her cunt was going to be his.

"What did you think about last night?" he asked, muttering the question against her pussy. He wasn't going to hide from her what happened in the club. He'd witnessed Holly's surprise and Mary's hurt by the claiming of women at the club. Raoul wasn't going to hide anything from Zoe.

Even if this is your one and only chance with her?

Raoul doubted he'd come to see her once he had her. He rarely liked to fuck a woman more than once. The club whores only held his attention because they knew what he liked and didn't try to hold back from him.

"You want to talk about that now?"

"What better way than when I've got you where I want you." He stroked his finger over her clit, watching her scream. "I can get you to be honest with me instead of trying to castrate me."

She laughed, and he loved the sound. In fact, he was starting to love quite a bit about her. Zoe licked her lips, pressing a hand to her head. "I hated that you were with another woman."

"What about the fucking? What did you think of that?"

"I didn't mind." He stared down at the evidence of her arousal.

"You don't look like you've got a problem with people fucking in public to me." He held his slick fingers up for her to see. "This is all the evidence I need." Raoul sucked his fingers into his mouth, moaning at the taste of her on him. "Fuck, you taste so good."

"You're doing this on purpose. I've never done anything to you." She whimpered, raising her hips up for him.

"You've been torturing me for months. Every time I thought about you, I got hard."

"I bet it didn't last long," she said, snapping the words at him.

"Wrong. I fucked those women, but they couldn't help me with my need. I wanted you, Zoe, only you. I didn't want anyone else. They were a means to stop me coming for you."

She placed her hands underneath her head to stare at him. "You shouldn't have gone to them. You could have come here. I wouldn't have turned you away, Raoul."

"You just made a big mistake," he said. Hearing that she'd welcome him wasn't something he needed to hear. The women at the clubhouse didn't satisfy him. How was he supposed to leave her alone now?

You're only going to be here the once.

Take what you want and enjoy it.

He didn't have to think about anyone else or anything, just this moment with the woman who'd been getting under his skin.

"I don't care," she said. "It's time I made some mistakes in my life." She cried out as he swiped his tongue through the whole of her slit. Her pussy was so wet and slick. Sucking her clit back into his mouth, he relished the exquisite taste of her cream, knowing he was becoming addicted to her.

"Then I'm going to be your first mistake." He pulled away long enough to rid himself of his jeans and clothes. Raoul pushed her up the bed, grabbing the condoms he always kept stashed on him. There were two condoms in each pocket of his jeans, and six in his jacket. He liked to be ready for whenever he wanted to fuck.

Throwing one condom on the bed, he wasn't about to scare her off with anymore than that.

She crawled up until she lay amongst the pillows.

"Are you always prepared?" she asked.

"When you're me you learn to be prepared for anything."

Zoe's smile caught at his heart, making him pause. No woman had ever left him feeling like this. She was one of a kind.

Drawing his thoughts back into focus, he climbed on the bed. She still wore the lace white bra that showcased her innocence. He wanted to rid her of all kinds of innocence and make her dirty, like him.

"You're thinking naughty things, Raoul."

"How would you know that?"

She glanced down at her bra then back at him. "I'm thinking naughty things as well."

Who was this woman in front of him? She was nothing like the woman he'd saved months ago. There was a siren locked away in there practically begging to get out.

"I don't just think naughty things, I do them."

"You're setting yourself up for a lot of promises here, Raoul. I sure hope you can keep them." She tilted her head to the side.

"What happened to the sweet little redhead?"

"Whoever said I was sweet?" She licked her lips. "I know I didn't. Don't assume to know anything about me."

She sat up on the bed sinking her fingers into his hair. Raoul didn't make her fight for it.

"You're a virgin, which takes all of your naughty thoughts and smashes them to smithereens."

"I may be a virgin, but that doesn't mean I don't want this." She slid her hand down his chest, stroking over the emblem of the Trojans MC. Most of the brothers had the emblem inked on their body somewhere. It was part of their initiation into the club, a show of loyalty. They mark their bodies with the club. Each person who was patched in would live and die by the club. "I've just never found a man I wanted enough."

"I'm not good for you."

"I don't care what you are or who you are. I want you." She ran her hand down until she circled his cock with her fingers. "Don't you want me?"

He was hard as fucking rock. There was no way for him to deny his need for her.

Emitting a growl, he tore into the condom, rolling it over his length.

"I want you, baby. I want you so fucking badly I can't even think straight. When I'm with those bitches in the club, I was thinking about you. I should be fucking castrated for what I want to do to you."

"You're not breaking any rules." She opened her thighs wide, and Raoul just couldn't take it anymore. He'd tried to be a good man, but Zoe was wrecking his mind in every way that counted.

Raoul slipped a finger through her core, testing to see how wet she was. When he took her virginity she was going to be in pain. He'd held Holly while he'd taken hers, but again, he hadn't given a shit about her whereas Zoe, he'd willingly die for her. He didn't understand his thoughts, nor did he care about them right in that moment. The only thing he cared about was getting balls deep inside her tight pussy.

Slipping between her open thighs, he gripped her hip with one hand, and with the other he guided himself toward her heat. He covered the condom in her cream, trying his hardest to take things as slow as possible. It was impossible to do when he wanted to ram home and take her cherry.

"I'm ready, Raoul."

Was she really ready for what he had to offer? He doubted she even knew what getting involved with him meant.

He couldn't hold himself back any longer. Placing the tip of his cock to her entrance, he stared into her beautiful eyes. She really was a beautiful woman, heartbreakingly beautiful.

****

Crap, shit, fuck, crap, shit, fuck.

Zoe wanted Raoul more than she wanted anything in her life, and she'd tried to put a brave face on it. Now, she was terrified. The tip of his cock rested against her entrance.

I want this.

Boy, did she want this.

Out of everything she'd been through in her life, this was something she really, *really,* did want, but what if it hurt?

All of her crazy thoughts rolled about together, throwing her this way and that. On the outside she looked calm and collected, yet her mind was running about screaming.

There wasn't any time to pull away as Raoul tensed up, sinking his cock deep within her. He pierced her virgin pussy, splitting her hymen and taking away the last shred of her virginity.

The pain was instantaneous. She tried to push him away, but he held her tighter against him.

"I've got you."

His voice didn't help to soothe her worries.

She kept trying to push him away and out of her. It was too tight, too big, and just too much.

"Please, I don't like pain. It hurts, please stop."

He caught her hands pressing them above her head.

"Stop fighting me. I know it hurts, but you also need to trust me."

Biting her lip, she stared into his pretty blue eyes. *Trust him.*

Raoul will keep you safe.

Out of everyone in her life, Raoul was the only one to keep her safe. She trusted him more than anyone in her life.

He held her trapped underneath his much larger body. She didn't fight him or try to get away.

"I trust you," she said.

The pain started to lessen between her thighs. Closing her eyes, she tried to think of something else.

"No, look at me, Zoe."

She opened her eyes to stare into his.

"I never wanted to hurt you."

Zoe smiled. "I know."

He didn't move an inch. The throbbing heat of his cock was still inside her. Taking a deep breath, she wriggled just a little.

Raoul hissed while she moaned. "I'm not going to be able to keep my word if you keep moving like that."

"I can't help it." She gasped out as he thrust a little more inside her. There was pain but nothing compared to the pleasure that exploded once again inside her.

"Fuck, baby, stay the fuck still."

"No." She wriggled her hips, trying to get him to create that amazing feeling.

She fought him in an attempt to get that pleasure once again.

He held her hands tightly, keeping her in place. In the process he pulled out of her only a little before sliding deep within her pussy.

Zoe moaned at the slightest of friction. Was she losing her mind?

"Please, do that again," she said, pleading with him.

He pulled out a little only to press back inside her.

"Yes, please don't stop."

"I'm not hurting you?"

"No." She tried to thrust up against him.

Raoul released her hands, gripping her hips. In three quick thrusts, he fucked her hard. She loved every second of it.

"No pain?"

"No." She shook her head. "It feels so good. Please, don't stop."

She'd gladly beg him to keep fucking her if it wouldn't take away that feeling again. His fingers dug into the flesh of her hips as he started to fuck her. The wet sounds of their body heightened her arousal. She reached up, touching his body, amazed that someone so fucking hot was in her bed, fucking her.

Raoul wasn't like any man she'd ever thought of herself with.

"Take your bra off. I want to see your tits bounce."

Her hands were shaking from the newness of being fucked. Raoul took over, lifting her up in his arms, flicking the catch of her bra. She moaned as he dragged the straps down her arms before throwing it away. In the next second his hands were cupping her breasts with his thumbs stroking over the tips.

"Fucking love these tits. I've been wondering what you look like. Would you have red or brown nipples, big or small?"

"You're not disappointed?"

"No, I'm fucking turned on." He pounded inside her, going deeper than ever before. "Touch yourself."

"What?"

He took her hand, placing it between her thighs.

"Touch your clit. Come all over my cock. I want to know how tight your pussy can get wrapped around my dick."

She stroked over her nub, screaming out at the intense pleasure of the moment. There was no end to the ecstasy that he created. No wonder Stacey loved fucking and the people she'd been around. This was amazing, fucking life changing.

With a few strokes over her clit she came apart, screaming Raoul's name. He didn't let her down.

His fingers held tightly onto her hips, and he fucked her harder than ever before. Raoul tensed above her, and his cock swelled inside her body.

She gasped at the tightness within her core. There would be bruises on her hips from the way he held her.

Raoul collapsed over her with his cock still deep inside her.

"Wow," she said.

"You've got no idea how fucking wow that really was."

"Really?" Zoe smiled up at him finally feeling shy. She'd just had sex for the first time.

"Baby, it was the best I ever had." He pressed a kiss to her lips. "You're going to be a little sore for a while."

He moved making her very aware of how sore she was going to be. "You weren't kidding."

She tried to hide her wince and failed.

"Oh, shit, I'm so sorry," Stacey said.

Zoe glanced over Raoul's shoulder to see Stacey and Landon staring at them. She screamed, realizing she was very naked and so was Raoul.

"Landon, if you want your vote you'll get your ass out of this apartment for the next couple of hours while I fuck my woman."

"Oh my God. Zoe, you go, girl."

She grabbed the pillows from beneath her even as her face flamed with embarrassment. "Leave, Stacey, please leave."

"You were the one who left the door open."

"We weren't really thinking about the door," Raoul said.

She slapped his arm. "Will you stop?"

"Get out now." Raoul's order sent them both running away.

"I can't believe that just happened."

"I can. I'll have to beat the shit out of Landon if he saw you naked." Raoul turned back toward her. "They probably both saw I was still deep inside you. I'd have loved to have gotten a picture of that."

"Of what? Their faces?"

He took the pillow from off her face. "No, the way your pussy looks with my cock inside you. You do realize I own you now. You're mine."

"No one owns me. I'm a free person."

"Not anymore." He kissed her lips, silencing any further protest. "There won't be anyone else, no men but me."

"Is this a biker thing? I thought bikers weren't into the whole possessive thing. I thought you liked sex with whoever would have you?"

"Would have us?" Raoul laughed. "Baby, there are a lot of people who'd give anything to fuck the men of the Trojans. We've had women come, sink to their knees and offer to suck our dicks, one by one."

"I'd never be one of those women." She shoved at his shoulder, but he didn't move anywhere.

"I know you're not like those women, Zoe. I wouldn't be here if you were like those women, and you'd have stayed at the party, joined in."

"Why didn't all the women join in?" she asked, curious.

"It was Daisy's scene. Just recently he's been fucking everything that walks. Don't know why and I'm not going to ask the brother. We deal with shit in our own personal way." He shrugged. "If he wants to be balls deep in a club whore then I'm not going to stop him."

"Are you going to be joining him in the fun?" she asked, stroking the chest that moments ago she tried to push away.

"That all depends?"

"On what?"

"On you. If you want this to continue and for me not to fuck club whores, then I won't. I'll stop. If, however, you don't want this to continue, I'll leave here and not come back. The decision is yours. I won't ever betray you, Zoe."

She believed him. It was strange this connection she had to him.

"Then I don't want this to be over after today. I want to be with you." She'd never been with a man, dated him, or done anything with one. Raoul wasn't just anyone.

"I'm yours, and you're mine."

"I can live with that." She smiled, wrapping her arms around his neck, and pulling him down to her. Zoe hissed as the pain increased just a little from his cock sliding in and out of her.

"Fuck, baby, you feel so damned good." He kissed her lips before going down to her neck, inhaling her sweet scent. "I can't take you again. I need to get rid of the condom and clean you up."

Zoe cried out as he pulled away from her body. The sudden withdrawal of his cock made her very aware of how sore she really was.

"Fuck me, there really is blood." Raoul stared down at the spot between her thighs.

"What is it?" she asked. When she looked down she saw the specks of blood decorating the lips of her pussy and some had fallen onto the bed. There wasn't a lot but enough to leave her embarrassed.

She scrambled off the bed, trying her hardest to clean the sheets away.

"Zoe," Raoul said, calling her name. At first she didn't want to hear him, but then he grabbed her arms, hauling her back. "Don't be embarrassed, baby. I like it. I know you're all mine." He kissed her neck, running his tongue over her pulse.

"Am I your first virgin?" she asked.

He tensed around her, and she didn't understand why.

"Yes, you're my first virgin."

She nodded her head, feeling special at his admittance. "I'm really sorry."

"You've got nothing to be sorry about. Let's not talk about it again. I'm happy to forget about it."

He walked her toward the bathroom. She shared a bathroom with her roommate. Most of Stacey's beauty products filled the counters in the bathroom. She watched as he filled the bath with some soothing salts, testing the water before he helped her inside.

"Thank you."

"I'll be back in a moment."

She watched his bare ass walk out of the bathroom. Zoe rested back in the bath, trying her hardest to relax.

I'm not a virgin anymore.

The thought alone made her smile. She wasn't a virgin anymore. Her obsession with Raoul had taken something she'd wanted to give to him.

One of the worst thoughts she'd had during her attack was those monsters were going to get something from her that she wanted to give to a man she cared about.

Moments later he returned. "I put the sheets away and remade your bed."

"You didn't have to do that."

"I wanted to do that." He climbed in the tub behind her, taking the sponge from her hands. "There's a lot I want to do for you, baby."

He started to wash her body.

Zoe couldn't believe this was really happening. The whole idea of Raoul being in her bed, or her bathtub, washing away the remnants of their lovemaking was too shocking for her.

Closing her eyes, she basked in his care, knowing in her heart there was nowhere else she'd rather be.

Chapter Five

Raoul was putting the finishing touches to his sandwich later that night when Landon and Stacey finally returned home. He saw Stacey was dead on her feet as she made her way straight to her bedroom. Landon didn't follow her, though. He came toward him.

"Busy day?" Raoul asked.

"You wanted her gone all day. She was kept busy. I don't think she'll be able to use her feet for some time."

He raised a brow at Landon's statement.

"I made her walk everywhere. I figured you don't want her asking too many questions, so I kept her busy. We fucked in a toilet when she started to ask about you. After that, I walked with her. I took her everywhere I went. Considering she's got a smoking hot body, she's really unfit." Landon thrust his hands into his pockets. "What's going on?"

"Zoe's mine. She's going to be under the Trojan protection as soon as I can get it sorted out." He needed time to introduce her to the club so the guys could assess her. Raoul wasn't going to have her as a club whore.

"Your old lady?"

"Yes. She needs to finish college first and get used to this way of life." Raoul ran fingers through his hair. Her innocence was a sore subject for him. When she'd asked if she was his first virgin, he'd wanted to tell her about Holly, but it just scared him. He didn't want her to not feel special to him. She was special in more ways than she realized.

"What do you want me to do?"

"You're her protection. I'm not going to be here all the time, but when I am, you can leave. I've got enemies, and if they find out about her, they will kill her." Being part of the Trojans didn't help him with enemies. The MC had a lot of enemies, but they also knew not to fuck with the club. Until Zoe was his old lady, living with him, and by his side, she wasn't safe. He wouldn't risk her life.

"I've got to keep fucking her roommate?" Landon asked.

"Or you can be friends with Zoe. She's a great friend, but you keep your hands to yourself."

"Zoe won't be friends with me. I couldn't even approach her without coming in with her friend."

"If you no longer wish to fuck Stacey then I'll talk to Zoe. She'll listen to me." Raoul cut the sandwich in half, giving a stern look to Landon. "She's my woman, but I don't want you spilling any club secrets, you hear?"

"Sure. I won't say anything."

"About anything." He didn't know everything the kid had heard. The last thing he wanted was for Zoe to be told the truth about him and Holly by anyone who wasn't him.

"I won't say anything. The club secrets are all safe with me. I promise."

"Good." Grabbing the plate, he made his way toward Zoe's room, kicking the door closed on his way past. He didn't even glance in to see if Stacey had heard anything of what he said.

Zoe was curled around a pillow with her leg thrown over the blanket, exposing all of her body. She was a fuller woman than most of the club whores, not as big as Holly, but she still had a lot of flesh for him to hold on to.

Placing the plate of food on the drawer beside the bed, he took a seat. Reaching out, he stroked out her curls, running the tips of his fingers down her face. She was so beautiful. Her red hair stood out against her pale skin.

All morning and afternoon he'd been fucking her sweet pussy, taking her to the brink of pleasure and shooting her over the edge.

The moment he stroked his finger over the curve of her breast, she started to stir.

"Come on, baby, it's time for you to wake up." He didn't want her to starve.

She moaned. "I want to sleep."

He chuckled. "I made you a sandwich, baby. It's time for you to eat, as otherwise I can't fuck you again."

Zoe groaned but started to sit up. "You're going to be cruel to me, aren't you?"

"No, I'm going to make sure you're cared for."

She placed the pillow in front of her body. He handed her the plate, watching as she lifted up one half of the bread.

"Can you cook?" she asked.

"No. I can't cook a thing, nor do I want to. This is the best you're going to get."

"I think it's perfect." She ate her sandwich while staring at his ink. "Did you always want to be part of an MC?"

"I didn't know what I wanted until I got to know the Trojans. Russ, he was the previous president, he showed me I could make something of my life. I didn't have to be a fucking punk to get what I wanted."

"You were a punk?"

"I was a piece of shit. That's what I was." Raoul took a bite of his own sandwich. "Russ gave me a chance."

"You were a piece of shit?"

"I stole, cheated, fucked up my whole life. I didn't have the best beginning, but I thought it meant I had a right to fuck everyone else up. Russ, he showed me another way. I owe my life to the Trojans."

"Why?"

"If it hadn't been for them, I would have been killed a long time ago." Raoul didn't like to talk about how he came to be a Trojan.

"I can see you're devoted to them."

"I am. I want to make this work between us, Zoe. I really do."

"Okay."

"Usually the women are kept close to the clubhouse. I'm not going to stop you from going to college. I need to think about how you're taken care of."

"Taken care of? I'm not going to do anything to hurt you or the club. I don't even know anyone."

He let out a sigh. "It's not about you. It's about me. I've got enemies, and so do the Trojans. I want Landon to be with you."

"He's dating Stacey."

"I've left the decision up to him, but I made sure Landon kept an eye on you before he came to the club."

She frowned, and he saw her working out exactly what he'd done. "You made someone come to protect me?"

"I made sure that you were taken care of. After what happened to you, I didn't want to risk it." He cupped her cheek, caressing her bottom lip. "I'll always take care of you. I don't care about your roommate, Zoe. I only care about you."

"I don't want Stacey hurt because of me. She really likes Landon."

"I'm not going to make him fuck a girl he doesn't want to. If he no longer wishes to be with Stacey, you've got to let him be your friend. I won't have it any other way."

"What happens if I say no?"

"Then you can finish college online. I'll take you back home with me. I won't have you in danger."

She took a deep shaky breath.

"I don't want to think about this. It's not fair." She placed her sandwich on the plate, putting it on the drawer beside her. "I didn't think this was going to come with complications." She drew her knees up to her chest, cutting him off from touching her.

"All I want is for Landon to be close to you. Nothing else. I promise."

"I don't want to have someone around me all the time. I don't want to do that to Stacey. If he doesn't want to be with her but he's always around me what do you think that's going to do? I need a roommate."

Raoul grabbed her hand but she tugged it away. "If Stacey leaves then I'll pay you for the room for Landon. How about that?"

"You'd trust Landon to live here?"

"Yes. I'd trust Landon with your life. This isn't about making life complicated." He placed his hand on her knee. "I'm taking precautions."

"By putting a guy in my apartment? What do you really think will happen?"

"Nothing may happen, Zoe. I'm not trying to scare you. The old ladies back at home, they're protected by the club. While you're at college, that protection is limited. Please, let me put Landon with you. It's for my own peace of mind."

She glanced over his shoulder toward the closed door. "I don't think I like him."

"Give him a chance. You don't have to like him. If he doesn't want to keep up fucking Stacey and she moves out, I'll move him in."

"I hate to say this, but I really hope he doesn't break her heart."

"Do you like her?" he asked. He'd not known if she liked her roommate or not.

"She doesn't drag me out of bed to rescue her from a club. I really hope it works out."

Raoul wished he could let her think the best of Landon, but he knew the younger kid was going to end things with Stacey. "I wouldn't hope too much. It would be worse if he gave her false hope."

"True. Wow, I lost my virginity and gained a bodyguard all in the same day." She lifted her shoulder. "It's not how I imagined the night of the whatever." She smiled, but it didn't reach her eyes. "So, what happens now? Do I wait for you to come around? How does it work?"

"First, you need my cell phone number." He held both of their phones in his hands. "I've already programmed my name in it. Call me whenever you want. Text whenever you want."

"Like a normal boyfriend and girlfriend?"

"Exactly. You don't ever have to be afraid to call me. I'd love to hear from you."

She bit her lip, staring down at her phone as if it was a deadly rattlesnake.

"What's on your mind now?" he asked.

"Nothing. Nothing. I'm just digesting everything that's going on."

"In a couple of weeks we're going to be having a barbeque at the clubhouse. I'd love for you to come and meet everyone."

"Okay."

"Also, you're going to learn how to shoot that gun," he said, opening her drawer. He pulled out the gun to check it over. It wasn't loaded, but she had the ammo beside the gun.

"I don't want to learn how to shoot. What if I kill someone?"

"Well, the aim is for you to either hurt, seriously injure, or kill someone. When you shoot a gun, that's all you're getting a chance for."

When he was satisfied with the gun, he placed it back in the drawer.

"Don't worry about a thing. You'll be able to handle anything."

****

The following week Stacey moved out of the apartment. Zoe watched her—she didn't know whether to call her friend or not. They hadn't been close, yet they'd shared an apartment together for over six months. Stacey didn't say anything as she packed her boxes up in a large pile.

Zoe kept trying to talk to her. "You don't have to leave."

"I really hope Landon makes you happy. He fucks like a machine."

"There's nothing between Landon and me. The guy is a douche."

"Hey, I'm sitting right here," Landon said, reminding both women that he was eating his breakfast. She hadn't seen Raoul in a week even though they texted each other constantly. Landon had broken things off with Stacey only to spend most of his spare time with her.

"Will you shut up? This is all your fault."

"What? I got what I wanted. I'm done, and it's time for Stacey to move on."

She wouldn't let him move in as Stacey moved out.

"I'll be out of your hair. I want the rent that I paid for this month."

Zoe had anticipated that and pulled the money out of her pocket. There was also a little extra because she felt bad about what happened between them.

"I'm really sorry."

"Don't be. I thought you were a virgin. I never thought you'd be a fucking whore."

Landon pushed his chair back from the table and walked until he stood in front of her. "You better back down and apologize. Zoe has told you nothing is going on between us, and she means it. I'm not fucking her. We're friends."

"Seriously, Landon, leave it," Zoe said, grabbing his arm.

"No, Raoul won't like it if I let this bitch call you names."

"So you're fucking both of them."

"Get the fuck out of this apartment, now!"

Even Zoe jumped at the sternness of his voice. Her heart started to pound inside her chest. The boxes were being taken down by a couple of guys Stacey had been with before Landon.

He took a step closer to her, grabbing Stacey's arm. "If you think of spreading shit around campus about Zoe, I will make sure you can't show your face again. Think about what you say when the boys that have already been between your thighs are helping you today. I counted at least six, but we both know there's nothing angelic about you."

Stacey turned on her heel, slamming the door behind her.

Collapsing onto the sofa, Zoe let out a sigh. "I hated that. It's not fair to her."

"She's a first class bitch. You don't have to worry about her."

Tilting her head back, she stared up at him. "What's going on at the club for him to be away for so long?"

Zoe didn't ask Raoul as she didn't want to come across as needy.

"Club business and I can't tell you everything that's going on."

"Great, back in the dark. Not a surprise."

"You were the one who developed your obsession."

"I know, and now I wish I hadn't." She ran fingers through her hair. "I've got to get out of here. I've got class in an hour."

"I'll walk you."

"No, no walking with me. I need to think. I've had too much of you right now." She grabbed her bags, passing Landon a key so he had his own. "I guess you can move your stuff in."

"Zoe, he wants to be here."

"It's nothing, Landon." She left the apartment, knowing in her heart that Landon would follow her.

Raoul had given him the instruction to protect her. She left her apartment and started walking toward campus. Checking behind her, she saw Landon was several steps behind.

"Come on," she said, hollering for him to join her. He ran the few steps, catching up with her. He wasn't even out of breath when he joined her. "I can't have you walking behind me. It freaks me out."

He chuckled.

"What are you going to do when you need to get to class?" she asked.

"We're on campus at the same time. I made sure to arrange my schedule around yours. I banged the secretary in charge, and she helped me to make the change."

"I really don't need to know that," she said, shaking her head. "Yeah, I've got the image of you screwing that woman. Isn't she married?"

"You'd be surprised how many married women want to fuck me."

"I'm not one of them."

"I know. It's kind of strange. You're the first woman I know that I had to work hard to get to know you."

"You're insane and crazy."

They talked all the way to her class. She wouldn't let him come in, but he pulled a book out of his inside pocket. It was a math study book. Chuckling, she left him to it while she sat through her English class. She loved English but didn't see herself having a career in the subject.

All the time she was making notes while the lecturer talked, she couldn't stop thinking about Raoul or Landon who sat out waiting for her. How was she to continue her life with a bodyguard?

The biggest question, what happens after college?

She'd not given this much thought at all. Raoul had come into her life, and now she didn't know what to do. The hour lecture was over, and she gathered up her paperwork as her cell phone went off.

Raoul: I'm waiting for you.

Leaving the classroom she saw Landon wasn't anywhere to be seen. She walked out of the campus, coming to a stop when she saw Raoul leaning against his bike

"Hello, beautiful," he said.

"Hello?" She stared at the bike before him. "What's going on?"

"I've been busy with the club, and I'd not forgotten you."

"Did Landon talk to you?"

"He didn't need to talk to me." Raoul held his arms open, and she stepped in without even trying to fight him. He tilted her head back, slamming his lips down on hers. "I couldn't leave. There was trouble with the Prez's woman. She had to go to the hospital, and we banded together to offer him protection."

"Just a precaution?"

"Yes. We have many enemies who'd use any chance to get back at us."

He rubbed her shoulders.

"I don't have classes tomorrow."

"I know. It's Friday. It gives Landon time to move into your apartment, and to study before I return you on Monday morning."

"Return me?" Her pussy grew slick at his words. Did he have plans? Would he fuck her again?

She'd tried to find release with her own hand, only to be left unsatisfied. Raoul had ruined her for her own hand.

"I want you to meet the club, and I want to make up for lost time." He reached around, grabbing her ass, and drawing her closer to him. The evidence of his arousal poked against her middle.

She moaned, cupping the back of his head. "Are you sure about that?"

"Yes. Climb on the back."

She put her bag over both of her shoulders, wrapping her arms around his waist. He gave her a helmet, and she glared at him. "What about you?"

"I don't need to wear a helmet. I know what I'm doing."

"If you know what you're doing, then what about me?"

"Better safe than sorry." He was always protecting her.

Wrapping her arms around his waist, he started up the engine. It wasn't long before the campus was far behind them. She saw the marker for the town of Vale Valley. Zoe squeezed him just a little tighter as he rushed toward town. Closing her eyes, she basked in having him between her thighs. She was nervous as hell being around the club, but for Raoul, she'd do it.

He slowed down as they came into the compound. Opening her eyes, she spotted several of the men who wore jackets similar to Raoul's. There were a couple of boys who didn't look old enough to be out of school wearing jackets with the word "Prospect" on the back.

Raoul tapped her leg, signaling for her to climb off. She did so only to fall to the ground when her legs didn't hold her up.

Tugging the helmet off, she looked up at Raoul, giggling. "You could have warned me."

"Are you all right?" He helped her to her feet, holding her close, and tapping down her body.

"Nothing is broken. The only danger is to my wounded pride." She gave him a pet lip. "They all saw me fall to my ass, didn't they?"

He looked over her shoulder. A smile decorated his lips a moment later.

"You're not wrong at all. They all saw you, and are now laughing."

She scrunched up her nose. "I don't know if I can face them." Zoe winced as he tugged the band out of her hair, giving her hair a little shake.

"Give them a smile, and they'll not mention anything. You look entirely fuckable."

"Do I?" She ran her hand up his chest.

He released a growl, and she gasped at the sound. Raoul squeezed the cheeks of her ass, bringing her tight against him. "Do you feel that?" he asked.

She nodded. There were no words to describe what she was feeling in that moment. "That's how badly I want to fuck you right now. If there wasn't a risk of someone seeing you, I'd have you bent over my bike while I fucked you. I don't care who sees that you belong to me."

She bit her lip, trying to fight the arousal that was growing deep inside her. Whatever Raoul was doing to her it was working. All she could think about was sex, fucking, and being his.

"Let me introduce you to some of the guys," he said. He placed an arm over her shoulder, grabbing her right hand, and locking their fingers together. She'd seen many of the guys do it on campus, but with Raoul, it seemed like a sign of ownership. He was letting all the brothers know who she belonged to.

They moved down the row of bikes to the one on the end. There was a brother on his knees, and he wasn't wearing a jacket. His display of ink showed him to be a member of the Trojans and not a prospect.

The moment he turned around she recognized him from the dance club all of those months ago.

"Daisy," she said. There wasn't anything that she forgot about that night. "I remember you."

He took hold of her hand, pressing a kiss to her knuckles. "Have you been keeping out of trouble?"

"I wasn't the one in trouble that night. I was in the wrong place at the wrong time."

"Yeah, sure. I believe you." Daisy looked at Raoul. "She yours or the club's?"

Zoe was confused by the question.

"She's mine. She belongs to me."

"Make sure the brothers know."

"I'm not doing it tonight."

"You're not allowed to do it straight away. The brothers need time to meet her, accept her. It's the way of the club. No one claims a woman without some getting to know her time."

The conversation went back and forth while she struggled to keep up. "I'm totally confused."

"Don't worry about it, honey. Club business." Daisy gave her a smile before turning away.

"This is how it's going to be now, right?"

"It's not that bad."

She didn't know how to respond to that and kept quiet.

Chapter Six

Raoul introduced her to Pie, Chip, Smash, Knuckles, and Bertie. From the blush on her cheeks she remembered Knuckles more than the others.

"You were the redhead who ran out of here a few weeks ago," Knuckles said, shaking her hand.

"Yeah, I don't like to, erm, to think about it." She stared at Knuckles's chest.

Kissing the side of her head, Raoul chuckled. "Don't worry about it, baby. Knuckles likes to show off. You'll be seeing a lot more of him in the future." While they were talking, Samantha and Baby came up to the men.

"Raoul, I've missed you. Are you going to fuck me at the party tonight?" Baby asked.

Gritting his teeth, he felt Zoe tense up beside him. This was the last thing he wanted to happen with her close to him.

"I've got company, Baby. Fuck off."

She pouted, running a hand up his chest. He released Zoe to grab her wrist. "I said no."

"If you're auditioning for another one of us, I can help."

"She's not going to be one of you," Raoul said. The brothers could watch all they wanted. He liked to be watched, but they were not going to fucking touch her. It had taken every ounce of restraint not to slam his fist in Daisy's face when he kissed her knuckles. They all needed to know to back the fuck off his woman. The time for sharing was long gone. The only one ever knowing the pleasure between her sweet thighs was him.

"You mean you're going to make her your old lady?" Baby whispered the words.

"Yes." He glanced toward Knuckles. "Take care of it."

"No, man, this is your problem. Not mine. This is something you need to take care of."

Grabbing Baby's arm, Raoul led her away from the group. In the background he heard Knuckles talking to Zoe, trying to distract her.

"What's going on? I thought you liked me."

Staring up at the ceiling, Raoul calmed down enough to deal with the woman. He didn't believe in violence against women, no matter how much they pissed him off. Baby had been a great woman to distract himself with, but even before he met Zoe, he'd known he wasn't going to settle down with a woman like Baby. Zoe was more his type than Baby was. He liked to fuck and he even liked to share women, but his own woman, he wouldn't share her.

"I didn't promise you shit, Baby. You're a club whore. You belong to the club and anyone who wants you. That's the way it works. You keep the men satisfied, and we give you a comfortable life." Their every wish was paid for by the club. The men made sure no one hurt the women that belonged to them. They took their role very seriously.

"I can't believe you don't want me. I've done everything for you."

"Baby, a club whore is never going to be an old lady," Holly said, walking into the clubhouse. Raoul hadn't heard her enter as he was too preoccupied with dealing with Baby.

He turned to see her in a maternity dress. Duke was standing behind his woman, gripping her shoulders.

"The rules are there for a reason," Duke said.

"What about Suz? She was a club whore," Baby said.

"She got knocked up. Broke the rules and if it wasn't for Crazy determined to look after his kid, she'd have left the club."

Raoul recalled the fiasco when Suz had announced she was pregnant. If the baby hadn't been Crazy's the whole club would have taken a DNA test to find the true father. It was a shame that Crazy got caught. Raoul hadn't liked the bitch even before she got knocked up.

"That kind of shit's not going to happen again," Duke said. "You want to become an old lady, you don't become a club whore first. Get the fuck out of my sight."

Raoul looked toward Zoe. Her eyes were wide as she took in the scene. This wasn't going how he thought it would be.

"Be careful with her. She's going to cause trouble if you're not," Holly said.

"You shouldn't be here."

"When Daisy called to say Raoul had brought a girl to the party, I wanted to meet her."

He tensed up. *Shit*. He'd lied to Zoe. He wasn't ready to tell her the truth or for her to know the real truth about his past with Holly.

Raoul decided he'd just have to take whatever was thrown at him. If Holly revealed the truth, then so be it.

"This is Zoe," he said, pulling her against him.

Holly smiled. "It's a pleasure to meet you. My mom's not here, but she told me how important it was to meet potential old ladies."

"It's, erm, nice to meet you."

"I won't be staying long. I've got an invasion growing in my stomach as you can see. Anyway, Mary should be back from her honeymoon, hopefully knocked up, and I won't be alone. She's my best friend."

Zoe nodded. "That sounds like fun."

Raoul squeezed her shoulder. "That's Duke. He's the club Prez now."

"Hello."

Duke shook Zoe's hand. "You're the one Raoul put Landon to work on."

She winced. "He didn't really work on me. He worked on my roommate, but yes, he's doing a great job of keeping me company. I'm sorry. I really don't know what to say right now. Are you like club royalty?"

Raoul pressed his hand across her mouth. "She doesn't know everything yet."

Duke burst out laughing. "You're rather refreshing," he said.

"I don't know if that's a good thing."

"It is."

Raoul squeezed Zoe's shoulder. Duke liked her. He saw it in the Prez's eyes, but he imagined it had more to do with Holly.

"So, what do you do?"

"I'm in college at the moment."

Raoul listened to her talk, surprised how easily she and Holly got on. Every now and then Holly placed a hand to her stomach.

"I'm sorry to be rude, but I think it's time I head home." Duke helped Holly out of the clubhouse. They all watched as Holly hugged several of the brothers on the way past.

"They all care about her, don't they?"

"Yes. Before Duke took over the running of the club, Russ was in charge. She's Russ's daughter. We've all kind of grown up together."

"Was Russ happy with her marrying someone who's older?"

"Yes. They're in love. No one can deny that. Duke would kill and die for her." The first one he'd already done, his own ex-wife.

"Wow, that's a commitment."

"Come on," he said, taking her hand.

"Where are we going now?"

"I'm going to show you to my room."

"Oh, you're going to take me to your room? What if we get in trouble?" she asked.

Raoul burst out laughing. She wasn't anything like he imagined. Zoe was playful in everything she did. It was refreshing; he did have to agree with Duke about that. Being around her was the first time he'd felt alive.

He walked up the several flights of stairs until he came to a stop outside his room. Pulling out a key, he unlocked the door.

"Why is it locked?"

"I've kept my promise to you to remain faithful. I have no plans to ruin it. If I don't lock the door, a club whore might come through. They'd been known to sneak into some of the brothers' rooms."

"Didn't you trust yourself not to follow through?" she asked.

"No. I trust myself to be faithful to you. I don't want anyone in my room. I never have." He opened the door allowing her to go inside. Each of the brothers had a separate bedroom in the clubhouse. It was easier if they ever went on lockdown. He really hoped they didn't go on lockdown anytime soon.

"I like your club, Raoul."

She walked toward the window, which overlooked the back of the clubhouse toward the large field out back.

"They're a great bunch of guys."

"And women."

He thought about Baby and knew she was going to be a problem. He needed to prepare Zoe in case Baby got to her when he wasn't around. "Baby would stab you in the back if she knew it would get rid of you."

"Do you mean with an actual knife?"

"No. She'd try to use any weakness against you."

"How can you have women like that hanging around the clubhouse?" she asked, tilting her head to the side.

"What do you mean?"

"You're telling me the woman will find a way to get rid of me, threaten me. How can you have them hanging around the clubhouse?"

"They're part of the club. Until you show yourself to be strong, Baby will try to take you down. I'm giving you a warning."

"A warning." She stepped closer toward him. "You're warning me? Why?"

"I don't want you to find any reason to leave."

"How are you going to get me to stay?" She ran her hands up the inside of his jacket, gripping his shoulders. His cock thickened, loving this teasing side to his woman.

Sinking his fingers into her hair, he claimed her lips, showing her with actions rather than words exactly how he was going to keep her.

****

Crazy stared at the clock on the wall getting pissed off. Strawberry wasn't the problem. He'd taken her to the park that afternoon, and for ice cream. Suz was supposed to be back by now. He was pissed off with himself, with Suz, too, but mostly with himself. Marrying the bitch and putting his name to hers had given the whore a sense of entitlement to piss him off.

She wasn't any better than the sluts at the club.

"Daddy, are you okay?" Strawberry asked.

"Yeah, honey, I'm okay." He wanted to wring Suz's neck. She was making him a laughingstock of the whole fucking club, and because of Strawberry, he'd let her do it.

A knock sounded at the door, and he went toward it. Flinging the door open, ready to beat the shit out of whoever opened the door, he reeled back when he saw Leanna. The moment she caught sight of his face, she took a step back.

"Erm, Suz called me. She said I needed to take Strawberry for the night." She didn't look at his face.

"Fucking bitch." He released the curse before he could stop. "I'm sorry. Come in."

She hesitated, staring at the door before looking at him.

"I'm really sorry for scaring you."

"Don't worry about it." She stepped into his home, and the moment Strawberry saw her, she charged at Leanna.

The smile that had been on Leanna's face returned.

"Hello, pumpkin."

"Hello, snuggles," Strawberry said.

Crazy's throat closed up at the affection between the two.

"You're staying with me tonight," Leanna said, placing Strawberry on the ground.

His daughter squealed, rushing toward the bedroom. "You don't have to take her."

"Suz told me you wouldn't be home and neither would she. I'd rather take Strawberry home than stay here. This isn't my place." She wouldn't look at him. Her arms were folded beneath her breasts, and he hated the fact she wouldn't look at him.

"I didn't know it was you at the door," he said.

"It's okay. We all make mistakes. I hope I never leave you feeling like that. You were kind of scary."

He doubted there was any "kind of" about it. Crazy had scared the living shit out of her. When he found Suz, he was setting some fucking ground rules. He was tired of this shit, tired of her. If he caught her with another fucking man, he was finished.

****

Breaking from the kiss, Zoe moaned, biting down on his lip. She pushed his jacket off his thick arms, relishing the feel of his hard muscular chest. The shirt that he wore was thin so it didn't mask any of his hard chest.

"I missed you this past week," she said, tugging his shirt over his head.

He shoved her bag onto the floor, followed by her jacket. Next he had her shirt over her head and flicked the catch on her bra.

"What are you doing?" she asked, moaning. He cupped her tits, running his thumbs over the peaks. She'd never considered herself to be so overcome by sexual arousal. A few moments with Raoul, and she was ready to fuck.

"We're going to play." He took hold of her hand, placing her palm on his chest. "Touch me, Zoe."

She caressed over his abdomen before moving up his chest, to touch his cheek. He cupped her breasts, bending down to take her nipple into his mouth. She gasped as he bit into her nipple, sucking hard.

Closing her eyes, she tried to stay still. Cream slicked her pussy.

Groaning, she tilted her head back, unable to hold herself up.

Raoul moved from one breast to the other, lavishing each hard bud with attention. She couldn't focus on anything. The pleasure was too much and yet not enough.

His fingers dug into her hips, going for the button that held her jeans up. In quick, jerky movements, he had her completely naked. He stepped back, and she opened her eyes as he removed his jeans.

The moment his cock was free it sprang forward, pointing up at her.

"Do you see what you do to me, baby?" he asked, taking hold of his cock. He ran his hands up and down the entire length. "This is what thoughts of you do to me. When you're not here, I'm fucking rock hard. This last week I've been beating myself off imagining myself inside you once again."

Zoe closed the distance, but instead of reaching out and touching him, she sank to the floor in front of him. "Let's give you something else to imagine," she said, gripping the base of his cock. Leaning forward, she flicked her tongue over the tip of his cock, where copious amounts of pre-cum eased out. She moaned at the musky, salty taste but didn't stop. Licking down each side of his cock, she got him slick with her saliva before taking the whole tip of him into her mouth.

Moaning, she took as much of him as she could before drawing away. Glancing up at him, she saw his eyes were wild. The lust blazed heat, sending goosebumps erupting all over her skin.

"You've got no idea what you're fucking doing to me."

She didn't answer, moaning as he wrapped her hair around his fist. He took control, drawing her close to his cock. She opened her lips, sucking him into her mouth.

"You look so beautiful, sucking my dick. You're completely naked. I could do whatever the fuck I want to you and no one could stop me. I brought you here tonight to claim you, Zoe. The brothers all know you belong to me. Duke was here to see that I'd brought a woman to take as my own. You're not a club whore. You're mine."

Each word he spoke only heightened her arousal further.

"No, don't close your eyes. Look up at me as you suck my dick." He touched her cheek, encouraging her where to look.

She didn't look away and took as much of his dick as she could. He hit the back of her throat, and she tried to swallow him down. Only when she gagged did he release her to pull away.

Bobbing her head onto his length, she loved the power she held over him in those simple moments.

"Fuck, yes, suck my dick, baby."

He thrust his hips, and she met those thrusts, loving the taste of him in her mouth.

All too soon, he tugged her head away, lifting her up into his arms. She was surprised at how easily he could throw around her size sixteen body. He threw her onto the bed, but he didn't let her go. Raoul placed her on her knees so that her ass was in the air. Before she could say anything, he slid his cock in deep. He was so big that she gasped at the slight pain his invasion caused. It had been a week since she'd last had sex, and her body hadn't the time to grow used to him.

"Fuck, you're so tight. I'm never going to get bored of this or of you."

She glanced over her shoulder to see him staring at where they were connected.

"So fucking perfect and beautiful."

He was a vocal man.

Raoul gripped her hips, slamming inside her, over and over again. He hit a spot so deep inside her that it was almost too painful for her. She screamed as he strummed her clit as he fucked her hard.

"You're not wearing a condom," she said, remembering he'd not taken the time to protect them both from pregnancy.

"I'll take care of it. You don't know how good this feels. Your pussy is so fucking slick and wet. I could stay here all fucking day." He slowed down his thrusts, taking his time to push in then out.

She stared back at him, seeing his gaze was still on his cock. Zoe jerked away from him when she saw he held a phone between them. That wasn't something she wanted to think about. She grabbed a pillow placing it in front of her. "What are you doing?"

"I was filming us together."

"Why?"

Zoe had heard many tales of how women ended up on some porn sites. They'd not talked about doing anything like that.

You're overreacting.

She doubted it.

"I want us to watch it." Raoul sat beside her. "We're doing this long distance thing—"

"It's not that long." She interrupted him in order for him to see the distance wasn't really a bad thing.

"Baby, when it's late, and we're both tired, we can watch this."

She stared down as he pressed play on the film. Zoe at first looked away. It showed his naked cock sliding in and out. There was only a minute's worth of footage, but it was enough to have her blushing.

"Watch us." He wrapped his arm around her shoulders, pulling her in close.

"I don't know if I can watch."

"I can. Your pussy is so tight. Look at me. I have to stretch you to get you open."

His cock did look huge as it slid in and out of her. Slowly, she started to get aroused. Their moans echoed around the room.

"I'm not ready for that yet."

"Okay. I'll put it away. I was only filming it for my own personal use. I wouldn't share it with anyone."

She believed him. He cupped her cheek, lowering her to the bed as he locked his lips with hers.

Moaning, she tried to turn to face him. He held onto her hip, keeping her in place.

"What's the matter?" she asked.

"Trust me." He rubbed his nose against hers.

Easing down, she stared up at him. He lifted her leg behind his ass, exposing her. She looked down to see him grip his still erect cock, placing the tip at her core. Raoul fed the tip of his dick inside her.

Gasping, she watched as his cock slid inside her core with ease. She was so wet that he didn't even need to play with her. When she was about to move her leg, he held her still.

"No, watch us together." She kept her gaze on his cock that was slick with her cream. His fingers glided over her clit, teasing her.

She couldn't handle the teasing for long. It had been too long since he'd touched her. Biting down on her lip, she tried to thrust onto his cock. He wasn't having any of it. Raoul slapped her pussy. "Don't fucking move. You're all mine, Zoe."

Nodding her head in jerky movements, she agreed.

He slammed inside her, stroking over her clit. She cried out, watching his cock that was so slick with her cream.

"This is how I want you, Zoe, soaking wet, begging for my cock."

"Yes."

"Let me hear you scream. I want you to scream for my dick."

Zoe couldn't keep the sounds from the lips a moment longer. Crying out, she exploded as her release took over, shaking the very foundations of her soul with how amazing it was. He drove his cock deep within her pussy and played with her.

Within minutes he followed with his own release, pulling out of her pussy and jerking his semen onto the lips of her pussy and stomach. When it was over, he leaned down, sucking her nipple into his mouth.

"I would never share a video like that with anyone, Zoe. I want you, and it would be ours."

She was panting for breath from the explosive orgasm.

"I know."

"Then let me film us together. It's what I want." He kissed up to her neck, sucking on her flesh.

"I don't know. What if something goes wrong? I don't want just anyone to see me." Zoe hated the thought of being laughed at.

"No one will know. It'll be between us. Give me this, baby."

Against her better judgment, she agreed, sinking against him. "I'm dirty."

"You're not on the pill?"

"No. I've never had a need for the pill before. I didn't see the point of being on it."

"I'm going to keep getting you sticky if we don't sort it out."

"I'll book an appointment and get on the pill." She ran her fingers across her stomach. "I'm sticky."

Raoul ran his finger through his cum, lifting it to her lips. "Taste me."

At first she wrinkled her nose. "I don't want to taste your cum."

"I taste yours."

She'd seen him licking his fingers clean. "What a way to make a girl embarrassed."

"There's nothing to be embarrassed about."

Opening her lips, she took his finger, tasting his salty essence. He rubbed his finger along her tongue, and all the time she stared into his eyes, swallowing him down.

He didn't taste bad at all.

"You're going to be the death of me."

Zoe didn't say what she was thinking. *You're the life of me.*

Chapter Seven

Raoul rolled Zoe over, kissing from her tits down to her stomach before landing on her pussy. He opened her thighs, teasing her clit into his mouth. They had yet to leave his room. The party was in full swing downstairs. The floor vibrated with the loudness of the music.

"Please, Raoul, let me come."

"I'll let you come when I'm ready to let you come." He slid his finger deep inside her pussy, relishing the sigh that came from her lips. Turning his finger, he stroked over her G-spot, watching the arousal heighten within her. "That's it, get close."

When she was on the verge of coming, he pulled out, pressing a kiss to her swollen clit. "Why are you torturing me?"

"I'm getting you ready."

"For what?"

"For us to go downstairs. I'm not going to hide the club from you." He licked his fingers clean, moving toward his drawers. Zoe had always been different, and he'd known it from the moment he first saw her nearly attacked six months ago. He picked out a pair of boxer briefs along with a shirt. "Put these on."

He tugged on his jeans and didn't bother with a shirt.

"I don't know if I can use my hands." She shook from the pleasure he'd given her.

Raoul took the boxers from her quivering hands, sliding the material up her thighs. She lifted up so he easily slid the boxers over her ass. He kissed her mound over the material. The musky scent of her arousal was easily detected. Raoul wanted to press his face against her mound and never stop licking her.

"I can't think when you do that."

Lifting her up, he slid the shirt down her arms, stroking over her tits as he did so. He left his jeans unbuttoned.

Taking her hand within his, he led the way out of his room. Part of him wanted to push her back into the room so she wouldn't see the other side of the party. Unlike Duke and Pike, he didn't intend for her to have the truth hidden away until the last minute.

Tell her about Holly.

He couldn't do it. Their relationship was still new, only a week old. Raoul knew in his heart that there was no other woman like Zoe out in the world. She'd come into his life and taken away everything else of any importance.

His only focus was on taking care of her.

"What is it?" she asked.

Raoul didn't even realize that he stopped on the stairs. "It's nothing."

Rounding the corner, Raoul pulled her against his side, refusing to let her go. The club was thriving with sexual activity. He saw Knuckles was getting his cock sucked by Baby as he watched the show by the pool table. Tori was being fucked by three men. Her screeching was already getting on his nerves.

"Okay, wow, this is nothing like the parties at campus," she said. "Yeah, totally lame ass parties." Cupping her ass, he held her tight to his side.

"No one is going to touch you. They wouldn't dare."

"Oh my, doesn't that hurt?"

Samantha was on her knees with Pie slamming his latex covered dick into her ass. These were the parties he'd once loved.

"It depends if he got her ready. Some women need to be aroused before they get fucked in the ass. Others, they can take it without any foreplay."

He found a seat next to Daisy and Floss. Both brothers weren't wearing any shirts and had their buttons undone, showing they'd already played a long time.

Zoe curled up against his side.

There were times he was amazed with how easily he'd adapted to having a woman of his own. Not so long ago he'd have pushed away any woman who curled against him like Zoe was now with her head resting on his chest.

"This is new for you," Daisy said, pointing down at Zoe.

She wasn't paying attention. Her gaze darted around the room taking in every deliciously sinful happening.

"Yes." He dared his brother to speak against what was going on.

Instead, Daisy threw his hands up. "You're the third fucker gone."

"Shut up." Raoul was gone, long gone of any fucking sense.

Kissing Zoe's head, he watched Crazy fucking one of the club whores on the stage. The sight shocked him. Ever since Crazy had been married, he'd not played or partied like he used to. From what Diaz told him, Suz was fucking anything with a dick, but Raoul didn't want to get in the middle of shit that happened with Crazy.

He wasn't called Crazy for nothing.

The bastard when angry went fucking crazy, insane crazy.

"What's going on?" Raoul asked, nodding at Crazy.

"He came in, grabbed one of the bitches off Knuckle, took her to the floor, and he's not let her go since. He's brought her off three times, and withheld her orgasm for the last hour. Something's on his mind, but I don't know what it is."

Crazy pulled out of Rita's pussy and slid his dick into her ass, fucking her with a ruthlessness that surprised Raoul.

Glancing down at Zoe's face, he saw she was turned on by the scene. Her nipples pressed against the front of her shirt.

"Do you like what you see?" he asked.

"I don't really know what I'm seeing right now. Is that his old lady?"

"No. That's Crazy, and she's one of the club whores." Raoul slipped his fingers under the material of the boxers finding Zoe soaking wet.

She gasped but didn't pull away from him.

"How do you become a club whore?" she asked.

"I thought you'd want to know more about becoming an old lady."

"What's the difference?"

"There's a huge difference." He slipped a finger into her tight pussy, groaning with the ease that she gripped him.

"Tell me." She sighed breathlessly, and he watched as Crazy pounded into Rita's ass. Something was clearly bothering him. He took his marriage vows seriously even if Suz hadn't. "Please."

"A club whore is voted in by several members of the club. She's fucked one after the other. We take her in turns, fucking her, sinking our dick into her mouth, ass, or cunt."

Zoe tensed. He pressed his thumb to her pussy to try to relax her. She eased against him.

"She becomes club property, pleases the men, and in return we all take care of them."

"Is she being initiated?" Zoe asked, nodding toward the pool table with Lori.

"No. There's only three men there, and in order for anyone to be initiated into the club, Duke has to be present or Pike. Neither of them are."

"How does Holly cope with that?"

"They don't have to touch the women. Duke gets the final say, and if he's not here, Pike deals with it."

Sliding his finger in and out of her pussy he knew Daisy and Floss were watching him. He didn't care. Her cream was the tastiest thing he'd ever had in his mouth.

"How did Holly and Mary become old ladies?" she asked. Her voice was a mere whisper combined with a groan at what he was doing to her slit.

"First, the men who want them have to be in love with them. At least that was the case for Pike and Duke. They both loved their women. Crazy, not so much." When his finger was soaking with her cream, he slid the digit to the puckered hole of her ass.

She tensed up, but he kept on talking in an attempt to distract her.

"There really are no rules for an old lady. It depends on the man. If he doesn't want to share her, doesn't grow bored, and is in love with her, then that's all they need to finally claim her."

"What happens for the club to know she's not to be touched?"

Raoul stared down into her hypnotizing green eyes. "Then she's fucked by that one person in front of the brothers, and they cannot touch. They cannot be part of it. That's what sets an old lady and a club whore apart in our world. Not every MC does it, but this is how the

Trojans work. If they're a club whore, anyone can fuck her. An old lady, she's not to be touched by anyone else."

He slipped his slick finger into her ass. Only the top of his finger and she tensed.

"You better get used to having this ass played with, baby. I'm going to be fucking it real soon." He kept playing with her while they both watched what was going on. Daisy and Floss moved on, finding one of the bitches that serviced the club. Crazy was finally spent and came to sit next to Raoul, swiping a beer.

"She yours?" Crazy asked, eyeing up Zoe.

"You can look, but you don't touch."

"Hands off, got it." Crazy held his hands up in the air before taking a sip.

"You've not fucked any other bitch but Suz since Strawberry was born. What's going on?" Zoe was not taking the whole of his finger into her ass. She squirmed by his side, but he could tell she was listening to him talk.

"Let's just say her days as my wife are numbered. I've got Diaz working on some proof."

"Dude, you could have gotten proof months ago. What's different now?"

"She was supposed to watch Strawberry for me tonight. Instead, I almost scared the shit out of my babysitter because Suz told her it was best for her to take my daughter. You should see Leanna and Strawberry together. They're more like mother and daughter."

Raoul took a sip of his drink. "What are you going to do?"

"First, I've got to find the proof I need to have leverage over Suz. I'm not going to kill her, but I need to make sure she can be silenced."

"Then what?"

"I'm going to give my little girl the mother she deserves. Leanna's days of being single are numbered, too. I've already had Diaz look into her."

Raoul frowned. "That's a little cold, isn't it? Using your babysitter to be a mother."

"She'll be getting me out of it as well. It'll be a mutually beneficial arrangement." Crazy got up from his seat, walking away from them.

"He doesn't even realize how cold he sounds," Zoe said, drawing his attention back to her, not that he could forget.

"No, he doesn't."

"Raoul, take me back to your room and fuck me. I can't take much more."

He didn't need to be asked twice. Removing his fingers, he wiped them on the outside of the briefs he'd put on her.

Zoe hadn't run away when he told her about the club. That was much better than Holly and Mary.

You've not told her about her not being your first fucking virgin.

Maybe he could get away with never telling her.
****

Zoe removed the shorts and shirt from her body as she walked to the bed. Raoul closed and locked the door.

"You did this on purpose," she said, sitting on the bed. "You made me so damned horny that I wouldn't care what you did to me."

She moved onto the bed, spreading her thighs wide.

"Do you have a problem with that?" he asked.

"No. I liked what you did."

Zoe watched as he kicked out of his jeans. His erect cock sprang free. The tip was slick with his pre-cum. She watched as he slid a condom over his cock.

"I don't want to take any chances tonight. I'm going to fuck you, Zoe, and fuck you hard."

"I'm waiting for you." She licked her lips watching his eyes flare. The lust shining in them reminded her that she was playing with a man of experience. In comparison to Raoul, she was a mere butterfly spreading her wings.

"Open your legs."

"I have."

"Wider."

She spread her thighs wide, lying back on the bed.

"Hold your legs open for me."

She cupped her legs under her knees, gasping as he dropped down so that his face was above her pussy.

"You look so fucking pretty." His tongue penetrated her pussy, sliding in but doing nothing in the way that his cock could do.

"Raoul?" She cried out his name as he flicked his tongue over her clit.

He lifted up and over her. His arm disappeared between them as he grabbed his cock. There was no time for her to get used to the feel of his cock before he slammed the entire length deep inside her. Raoul was not small or slender but thick and long. She panted for breath. The pleasure and pain masked everything in her mind. She didn't know if she was to enjoy it or hate what he'd just done. He pulled out until only the tip remained within her. She stared into his eyes as he slammed back within her. Over and over, he slammed every inch of his cock inside her, going deeper than ever before.

Zoe couldn't contain her screams as he took her to the peak but still didn't allow her over the edge.

"Please stop tormenting me." She begged and pleaded with him to stop but not to stop. Zoe didn't want the pleasure to end. She wanted to come.

"You'll come when I give you permission to come. Not a moment before."

She cried out as he pulled all the way out of her body. In quick easy movements, he flipped her onto her stomach, and pushed a couple of pillows beneath her hips, raising her up a little.

Zoe didn't have the chance to understand what he was doing before his dick was back to pounding inside her.

Clawing at the bed, she lost focus.

"You're all mine, Zoe," he said, kissing the back of her neck. He wrapped her hair around his wrist, tugging on the length. "I'm going to spend every chance I get fucking you. You're fucking perfect for me."

She listened as his lips slapped against her ass.

"I'm going to fuck your ass one day, Zoe, get you all nice and ready to take me. I'll own every single part of you. That's what will make you an old lady, Zoe. You'll only ever know my cock."

Raoul didn't let up in his thrusts, pounding away inside her. The hand holding her hair, tilted to the side as he thrust his other between her thighs. "Come all over my dick, Zoe."

There really was nothing left for her. He'd kept her at the peak of pleasure for hours. With a few strokes of his fingers, she came apart, seeing stars before her eyes.

"That's it. Fucking perfect. Perfect cunt. All mine."

His words ran together. She didn't make any sense of them.

He pulled out of her pussy at the last moment, tearing the condom off and jerking his seed all over her ass. She didn't move as he collapsed beside her. He cupped her hip, kissing the back of her neck.

"You really need to get on the pill."

"You could have finished in the condom." She pushed some hair off her face, glancing at him over her shoulder.

"I needed it."

"Why?" Heat filled her cheeks as he caressed down her back until his fingers smeared in the natural lubricant.

"I wasn't making it up. I'm going to fuck your ass, but I don't have any lube upstairs." He gathered his cum onto his fingers, working them at her ass.

She tensed up.

"I'm clean, and I know you are. I promise you, Zoe, I'd never put you at risk."

"I don't know if I want you to fuck me there."

"Let me show you how good it can be."

"You're not trying to change my mind?"

"I'm always going to try and change your mind. I know what I like, and I know what I can give you."

Licking her dry lips, she nodded. "Fine. Who am I to argue with the master?"

"Master? I like that."

She burst out laughing only to stop as his finger stroked over her ass, going across the puckered hole that, to her, was forbidden.

"I'm just going to get you nice and slick. You know, in the olden days men used to fuck women in the ass just so they couldn't get pregnant."

Rolling her eyes, she chuckled. "That's not true."

"Sure is. Or, at least I think it is."

"You're a history buff?"

"No. Not a chance. I'm a sex buff."

"Well, this is the modern world. If I don't like it we can use the old fashioned method if you don't want to wear condoms."

"What's that?" he asked, kissing her shoulder.

"The old fashioned method?"

"Yes."

"We don't have sex."

"I'm good with condoms. I like modern methods just like every other modern man." He kissed her neck, nibbling over her pulse. "But I hope you like the old fashioned way for not getting pregnant."

"Why?"

"I love your ass, and there's going to be nothing better than watching you come while I ride it."

"You're bad."

"No, baby. You've not seen bad. With you I've been fucking saintly."

She stopped chucking as the tip of his finger pushed into her ass, going past the tight ring of muscles. Zoe gasped, making him stop with her hand up. "Please, stop."

"What's the matter?"

"It burns."

"I'll take it slower." He pushed his other hand under her neck, moving down to cup her breast. He pinched her nipple, bringing another gasp from her. "I told you I want you to like this."

She didn't argue or fight with him. The last thing she wanted to do was fight with the man who had a finger up her ass.

Swallowing past the painful lump in her throat, she tried to relax. In and out he pumped his finger, using his semen as a lubricant on her flesh.

"I'm not going to play for much longer. I don't want to hurt you."

"Okay." She nodded even as he increased the pace of his finger. He rimmed her ass with a second digit but didn't thrust it inside her, which she was thankful for. She couldn't handle a second finger just yet.

He didn't stop immediately though. Raoul kept working her ass with one finger, and she was shocked after several minutes to find a spark of arousal start to ignite within her.

"That's it. I know you feel it, Zoe."

"What?"

"Your pussy has just gotten wet. You want this now."

"How do you know?" She frowned. He wasn't anywhere near her pussy.

"You've started pushing back against my hand. You want me to fuck you, take you harder than ever before. I won't, not tonight."

He slid the second finger inside her, taking her completely by surprise. She didn't try to fight him, welcoming the sudden burn and fullness it created.

"Yes, yes, yes," she said.

"Touch your clit, Zoe. Come for me."

It was her turn to reach between her thighs, stroking her pussy. She teased her clit like he'd shown her, giving herself pleasure. He kissed her neck, finger-fucking her ass at the same time. With her other hand, she reached for his cock. The angle was awkward, but she started to work on his erect cock, moaning as he surrounded her.

This was an entirely heady experience, one she couldn't wait to repeat.

"Come, Zoe."

Her body was no longer her own but Raoul's to command all of his own.

She came apart, riding his fingers. He groaned in her hair, and more of his cum landed on her back. When it was over, they were both panting for breath.

"You're going to fucking kill me, Zoe."

He withdrew his fingers, and she released him. Raoul didn't give her any reprieve, lifting her up into his arms, and carrying her through to his bathroom. He ran them both a bath, not letting her go. Zoe was thankful in that moment. She couldn't have handled being alone right then.

She climbed into the bath as Raoul settled behind her. He washed his fingers before touching her. Instead of being disgusted she found the action incredibly sweet.

"I've got you. I'm not letting you go."

"What do you plan to do with me?" she asked, locking her fingers with him.

"What do you mean?"

"You mentioned about me being an old lady. How does that work?" She rested her head on his chest.

"I want you to be my old lady. I want you to meet Pike and Mary, spend a bit more time at the club, and then I want to claim you as my old lady."

"I don't want to stop going to college."

"I'm not going to stop you from doing anything that you want to do."

She nodded. "I can still go to college while I'm your old lady?"

"Yes."

"You don't think it's too soon?"

"No. I want you, Zoe. I've not been able to stop thinking about you since that night I first met you. Even with those bastards holding you down, I knew you were different, just by looking at you. You weren't like any woman I'd seen."

She closed her eyes, suddenly feeling tired.

"Zoe," he said, waking her as she started to fall asleep.

"Yes."

"Will you be my old lady?"

She laughed. "Yes. I'll be your old lady."

She didn't know if he said anything else to her. Exhaustion finally took over, and she fell to sleep with his arms wrapped around her.

****

The following afternoon Crazy pulled out his cell phone to see Diaz was calling. He watched Strawberry and Leanna having fun at the park. Neither of them knew he was there, and he didn't want them to just yet. He wasn't going to make a quick decision with Strawberry's care at stake.

Leanna was a good woman, a caring woman, but did she want kids?

Strawberry slid down the slide, rushing toward Leanna, laughing. To any stranger looking on, they appeared as mother and daughter. The sight alone broke his heart. Suz would destroy that little girl if he let her, and the last thing he wanted was for Strawberry to suffer.

"What do you have for me?" he asked.

"Your wife has been a busy little bee, Crazy. I'm surprised you've not discovered what she's up to."

"Just give it to me."

"She's going to be in a heap of trouble with the cops if they ever get wind of this shit, Crazy."

"I don't give a fuck. What I have, will it keep her mouth shut and out of my life?"

"The shit I have, it's going to have her begging you for mercy."

"Good. That's exactly the way I like it."

Diaz gave him a rundown of everything Suz had been up to. By the time he was finished, Crazy was struggling to keep in control.

"Are you sure?"

"Dude, I'll email you everything. I swear there's nothing wrong in this information."

"Email me everything and send files my way. Meet me at the clubhouse barbeque in a week. I'll pay you then."

Disconnecting the call, he rang Duke immediately. He wouldn't do anything that would blow back on the club.

"What's the matter, Crazy?" Duke asked.

"Suz. I'm going to divorce her. I want her out of the club business and away from my daughter."

"That's pretty fucking dangerous. You know she knows club business."

"But I've got shit that will put her ass in jail for good." He told him about the arrangement he had with Diaz.

"We'll have a club meeting immediately after," Duke said. "This shit better not hit the fan, Crazy. I'm all for getting rid of Suz but not at the risk of the club."

"I'll kill her if I have to." Crazy didn't like killing women, and with Julie gone it would put the heat right at their doorstep if another wife was to suddenly go missing.

"Fine."

He disconnected the call as Leanna was walking with Strawberry out of the park. No longer wanting to be invisible to the woman, he stepped into her path. She paused, shocked. When she looked up, he saw that first flash of the fear that she'd had last night.

"Hello," she said.

"Daddy."

He bent down, picking up his little girl.

"Hello, precious. How was your morning?"

"Great."

"How about I take you and Leanna out for lunch?"

"No, you don't—"

"I'd love that."

Leanna wouldn't argue with his little girl. She wouldn't do anything to hurt another living soul, unlike his current filthy wife.

"Then I'd love to come. If I'm not intruding?"

"You're not intruding at all." He led the way toward the diner. If he was going to make Leanna a permanent part of his life, he needed to get her used to his company. At any moment she looked like she wanted to run for the hills. He couldn't have that.

Chapter Eight

"What the hell is this?" Zoe asked the moment they entered her apartment. Landon was standing there playing pool as they entered. No one else was in the apartment, which Raoul was thankful for. He doubted Zoe would handle a string of girls coming and going. Before paying Landon's rent, he'd given him a warning to keep the women quiet or to take them somewhere private.

"It's a pool table. What do you think it is?" he asked.

"What's it doing in the sitting room? Where's my coffee table?" She dropped her bag to the floor, and Raoul closed the door.

"I got rid of it. Actually, the piece of shit furniture broke so I replaced it with something way cooler, don't you think?"

"This is not way cooler. This is an invasion of my home."

"I live here as well. We rent this apartment together." Landon moved to the far wall, offering her a pool stick. "Come on. Have a game. It will be awesome."

Zoe shook her head. "No. I need to take a shower and study." She turned to glare at Raoul. "You better figure this out. Otherwise he's gone."

Raoul watched her disappear into the bathroom, before her very swift exit was hindered by the fact she didn't have a change of clothes. She shot him a glare before going into her bedroom, coming out with a change of clothes. Every time she slammed the door, he marked it down for the number of times he was going to spank her. The bathroom door slammed for a second time. He was going to spank her three times, twice for the bathroom, and once for the bedroom.

Taking the pool stick from Landon, he shot a ball. Neither of them played any real game as they took it in turns to shoot the ball into the holes.

"How was the party?" Landon asked.

"Great. Did you have trouble moving in?"

"Nah, it was fucking easy. Zoe doesn't keep a lot of shit around. Did you know all that cosmetic shit in the bathroom was Stacey's? I think Zoe had a razor, soap, and some special hair shit." He shrugged. "I've got more in there now."

Raoul snorted.

"What? I've got to keep my good looks up. Women don't fuck me for nothing."

"I doubt any of the women would fuck you if they knew how vain you were."

"I'm taking one for the team." Landon chuckled. The moment he finished college he'd be prospecting full time for the club.

"Zoe's going to be my old lady. I'm going to need you here to keep an eye on her."

"No problem with me. She's a cool chick, can't stand my guts for anything but friends. I'll take care of her."

"Hands off, Landon, I mean it."

"Fine, hands off." Landon held his hands up. "I won't fuck her, brother."

"I won't fuck you either," Zoe said, walking out of the bathroom. Her hair was wet from the shower, and her cheeks were flushed. She didn't pay them any more attention, entering the kitchen to put the kettle on. Out of the corner of his eye, Raoul watched her move around. He wished Landon wasn't around. The thought of leaving her left him with a heavy feeling in the pit of his stomach.

"I've got to be heading back," Raoul said.

"Fine. I'll get Zoe to play."

"I'm studying, Landon. You can play by yourself."

Raoul threw the pool stick onto the table, reaching for his woman. He pulled her close to him, inhaling the fresh fragrance of her soap.

"I'll call you."

"Okay."

He slammed his lips down on hers, taking the kiss he didn't want to end. When it was over, he let himself out of the apartment. He climbed onto his bike, riding back to Vale Valley. Not once did he look back. Leaving her behind was already hard enough. He didn't want to keep doing it.

Daisy was working on his bike when he drove into the clubhouse parking lot. It was only lunch time, but if he'd stayed with Zoe, he wouldn't have wanted to leave.

"What's going on, brother?" Daisy asked.

"Nothing. I'm just trying to work through my shit. You know how it is."

"Zoe handled the club a lot better than I thought she would."

"I've told her how to become an old lady, and that I intend to make her one."

"And you're still dating?"

"We're still dating. She's finishing up college. I wouldn't take that away from her."

"You're not that much older than she is, Raoul. I wouldn't worry. It's not like you're in your forties."

Raoul tilted his head to the side. "You're in your mid-thirties."

"So?"

"This pussy you can't have, who is it?"

Daisy completely shut down, a blank expression on the whole of his face.

"That's not your business, and I'd appreciate it if you stayed out of mine," Daisy said.

He chained his bike up but didn't budge. "What pussy has got you screwing everything that walks with a vagina?"

For several moments Daisy didn't speak. "My sister's best friend." The words came out of his mouth as a mere whisper that if Raoul hadn't been listening he wouldn't have heard it.

"What?"

"I went home over Christmas and New Year. My sister was home from college with her best friend." Daisy ran the dirty cloth over the body of his bike without looking up as he spoke.

"Do we know her?"

"No. The folks don't want nothing to do with the club I'm with. I go to visit my mom and sister, not my dad." Raoul had known there was no love lost between father and son with Daisy. He despised his old man.

"Anyway, let's just say little Maria has all grown up." Daisy threw the cloth to the ground. "Leave it, and if I hear any shit from the brothers I'm coming for you."

"I won't say anything."

"Good. Look, she'd never look at a guy like me. I'm fucking old, and she wouldn't even look at a biker, okay? She's one of those innocent types who wants kids, a husband, to settle down."

"Well, shit, I didn't figure you for someone who can read minds as well."

"I'm being fucking serious here."

"I'm not saying anything. You clearly know what you're talking about." Raoul held his hands up. He'd never expected Daisy to open up to him.

They both stopped speaking as Duke's large truck pulled into the parking lot. Raoul went to Holly's side, helping her out of the truck.

"I can do that. I'm not a total invalid. I'm pregnant, remember?" She snapped each word at him.

Raising a brow Raoul looked toward Duke.

"Hormones." Duke spoke the word without making a sound.

"Pike and Mary are due back today. I refuse to spend another moment spread out on the sofa. I want to see my best friend," Holly said.

"They're back today? I didn't know they were back today," Raoul said.

"Mary's had no choice but to come back," Holly said, smirking. "Pike knocked her up, and the morning sickness is not making the trip enjoyable for either of them."

Raoul burst out laughing. The two best friends were knocked up together.

"You can laugh all you want. Wait until your woman is like this," Duke said, warning him.

"Not going to happen to me," Daisy said.

Raoul didn't say anything, but he imagined Maria was only going to be safe for so long before Daisy got his head out of his ass and claimed her. Entering the clubhouse, he went straight for the bar. He pulled out his cell phone to see several texts.

Landon: Zoe's an alien. She's trying to get me to sell the pool table.

Zoe: I'm not having a pool table.

Landon: She's completely insane.

Zoe: Raoul, I mean it, talk to him.

Laughing his ass off, he took the drink from Baby. She was staring at him sweetly. He stared down into his coffee, suspicious. Placing the cup on the counter, he saw her face fall.

"What the fuck did you do to my drink?" he asked.

His voice rose enough to grab everyone's attention.

"N-nothing." She stuttered the word, turning red as he continued to glare at her.

"Don't fucking lie to me," he snarled out, ready to commit fucking murder.

Duke stepped up to the counter. "What's going on?" he asked.

"Baby's put something in my drink. I don't know what it is." He kept glaring at Baby, watching her eyes fill with tears. Her mascara started to run down her cheeks, sniffling. "What the fuck did you put in my drink?"

"I'm sorry. Suz said it would work."

The mention of Suz had Duke tensing.

Holly placed a hand on his back. "What the fuck does that slut have to do with this?"

"It's just to help him relax."

"Why? Why the fuck would you need me to relax?" Raoul asked. If it wasn't for the counter between them, he'd be choking the life out of her.

"I know," Daisy said. "If she can get you to relax and fuck you without a condom, she's at risk of getting pregnant, isn't that right?"

Baby nodded, sobbing into her hands. "Suz said it worked for her and that she had the best of both worlds."

"It's not going to work for me, you fucking whore," Raoul said, grabbing the cup, and throwing it against the wall. He was so fucking angry. "I've got a woman of my own. What the fuck does it take to prove to you bitches your place?"

Duke placed a hand on his shoulder. "Enough. Daisy, put Baby into lockdown. I don't want her to be able to connect with Suz or anyone else. I want to get to the bottom of this. Raoul, call Crazy. I want him here."

Raoul stared at Baby. He'd heard the order from Duke, but he was going to make sure Baby understood the shit she'd just done. The moment she was free from the counter, he snatched her out of Daisy's hands, slamming her against the wall. He wrapped his fingers around her neck. "Let's make one thing clear." In the background he heard his brothers shout at him to stop. He didn't, and was going to make everything clear to her. "I promised Zoe I'd remain faithful to her, and I'm not going to break my promise. If I'd taken that drink and woken up beside you, naked, even if I let you live and you came to me pregnant, I would have killed you and buried your body so Zoe wouldn't ever have known. I don't make a habit of killing women, but you wouldn't have been a woman, Baby. You'd have been my enemy, and those I kill without remorse."

Terror shone in her eyes, and he threw her back into Daisy's arms. If he touched her again, he was going to kill her. Storming out of the clubhouse, he dialed Crazy's number, giving him the lowdown of what was going on.

Once he finished, he turned around only to stop when he saw Holly.

"Hey, you," she said.

"Hello." It was the first real time she hadn't looked at him with anger.

"You really do care about Zoe. The woman you brought to the party at the weekend?" She folded her arms over her stomach, highlighting how big she'd gotten. "Please, don't stare. I'm the size of a tank, and the insecurity I'm dealing with right now is a fucking bitch."

He chuckled. "I love her, Holly. I never thought I'd meet someone who makes me feel like this."

"Makes you feel like what?"

"She's the only thing in the world that I care about. It's unlike anything I've ever felt."

She smiled. "I feel that way every time I'm with Duke. When we're not together, I think about him all the time."

Raoul nodded. He stared down at his cell phone, wondering what Zoe was doing at that very moment.

"Don't let her get away, Raoul. We're lucky to have found someone we love more than anything in the world."

He agreed with her.

****

"It's not you, baby, it's me. I'm not ready to settle down. I'm a sucker for a pretty face. I'm broken inside, and you can't fix me."

Zoe snorted as Landon continued to sweet talk the girl he'd brought over last night to fuck. She'd spent the whole night listening to him pounding the bed against the wall. At two in the morning she'd gotten so tired, she'd stuck her earbuds in, and listened to music.

The door closed.

"I don't know who I feel sorry for, you or that poor girl."

"Why feel sorry for her? She got the banging of a lifetime, and I got a hundred bucks."

"Why did you get a hundred bucks?" She frowned, holding her hand out. "Wait, I really don't want to know."

"Don't worry, I'll tell you anyway. There was a bet going on to see who could get into Heidi's pants first. I won, so the money is mine."

"Ew, you actually have bets on for screwing girls on campus?" She wrinkled her nose hating her peers more and more. At least Landon hadn't brought any of his male friends to the apartment. She would have been pissed to discover those kinds of men at her apartment.

"There's a thousand dollar special if a guy gets with a teacher."

"You see, this is the reason I never wanted to have a male roommate. You guys are disgusting."

"Why are we disgusting?" he asked. "That girl left with several damn good orgasms. I also didn't film it, and some of the guys do."

"What?"

"Exactly. I'm not the worst choice for a sex partner. Some of the guys like to torment the girls afterwards with their conquests. It's cruel really, but there's nothing we can do about it."

She shook her head. "I can't be thinking about this right now. I'm studying." It had been three days since she last spoke to Raoul.

"What? Don't you want to know what the guys thought about you?"

Frowning, she glanced over at him. "They had me down for money?"

"Yes, the virgin. You were worth five hundred bucks."

Zoe didn't know what to do or say. On the one hand she was pissed off that they would bet on her. On the other, she really didn't care.

"Don't worry. I warned them if they tried to continue the bet with you, I'd hurt them."

"Why would you do that?"

"I did it on behalf of Raoul and the club. No one takes the piss out of an old lady."

"I'm not an old lady yet."

"You will be. All I care about is you've been claimed by Raoul. I'll look after you and take care of you."

She stared down at her English book, but her mind wasn't on the words written on the page. Her thoughts were on Landon and what he'd just said to her.

"Why do you want to be a Trojan so bad?" she asked.

"They're the best biker club around. I could have joined with The Skulls or Chaos Bleeds, but I didn't want to. I like the Trojans. They're fun. The other two clubs always seem to be in a shitload of danger."

"Danger?"

"Yeah, clubs like that, it creates enemies. It's why Raoul wants you protected while we're here. Each club has their own set of enemies. With me here, I can protect you."

Zoe hadn't really given it much thought about what it meant joining the club.

Her cell phone pinged, and she saw Raoul had texted her.

Raoul: Miss u. How's studying?
Zoe: Fine. Landon's being a pain in the ass.
Raoul: What are you doing?
Zoe: Studying. Wishing you were here to distract me.

"From that smile on your face I'm guessing it's Raoul texting you," he said.

She didn't receive another text immediately after so she put her phone down. "Don't you hate the fact girls are using you for sex?"

"Baby, I don't have any problems with the girls using me for sex. I live for it. I relish it."

"I don't know. I imagine you must get lonely at times." She stared down at her book.

"Why would I get lonely? I have all the women in the world falling at my feet."

"Yeah, but are you really happy with that? I mean, you've got all of these women, Stacey, for instance, was she the only one you took the time to fuck?"

"I only slept with her in order to get closer to you," Landon said.

"That's not a good enough argument. That girl you've just ushered out of the apartment, how many times have you slept with her?" When he didn't answer straight away, she gave him a stern look.

"What? I slept with her once. Once is enough."

"Why? Afraid your technique might not be all that great?"

"I've no idea what you're trying to say, but I can promise you, it's nowhere near the truth."

"Really?"

"Yes, I'm awesome in the sack. I've got girls begging for a chance to fuck me." Landon looked proud of his achievement.

Tilting her head to the side, Zoe picked up her pen, running the bottom against her lip.

"What?" he asked, after a few seconds' worth of silence had passed.

"Nothing. I was just wondering out of all of those girls who want a chance in your bed, how many of them are actually running for a second chance. I don't see them knocking down our door to get to you." She folded up her books, getting ready to call it a day.

"What the hell do you mean by that?"

"They're always happy to sleep with you, but they're not knocking down your door for a second go. I think you need to consider that before you call yourself good in the sack."

She left him alone with her parting words.

The moment she closed her bedroom door, her cell phone rang.

"Sorry about that, babe. I had business to attend to," Raoul said.

"That's okay. I was just messing with Landon's head. He really does think he's God's gift to women. I was just proving him otherwise."

"I hope you're not trying to cause trouble."

"Me, trouble? I don't have the slightest clue what you mean."

Raoul laughed. The sound thrilled her. "You know exactly what I mean. How's college?"

"It's boring. Before I met you I used to think it was amazing and I couldn't imagine doing anything else with my life. Now, it sucks, big time."

He nodded. "Does that have to do with me?"

"Yes, it does."

She settled on the bed, resting her hand on her thigh. "I miss you, Raoul. I need you."

Raoul groaned. She heard him moving then the sound of a door locking closed.

"Where are you?" she asked.

"I just went up to my bedroom. Where are you?"

"In my room. The door is locked." She bit her lip while stroking her thigh. "I really wish you were here."

"Baby, I'm right here. Touch yourself."

"What?"

"You heard me. Slide your fingers into your pants and let me know how wet you are." At first, she hesitated, not wanting to take that final step.

Why not?

She couldn't argue with her own need. Raoul wasn't here, and this was the next best thing. Sliding her hand into her pants, she gasped the moment she touched her clit.

"How wet are you?" he asked.

"Very wet. You wouldn't need to get me ready for you, Raoul. You'd slide in so easily."

"Press a finger inside that little cunt."

She did as he asked, moaning.

"Is your pussy tightening around your finger?"

"Yes." She shouted the word not caring if Landon heard her. This was the best pleasure she'd gotten in days. Raoul had turned her into a sex starved woman, only capable of reaching climax with him.

"Add a second finger. I want to hear you screaming my name."

"Raoul, I wish it was you. I wish it was you here right now touching me."

"You're not the only one who wishes it, baby. Fuck, I'm rock hard right now. My hand isn't good enough. I want your wet pussy sliding over my cock."

"I went to the doctors, Raoul. I'm on the pill. We've got two weeks, and then we can fuck without a condom."

"I can fuck my cum into your sweet pussy."

She cried out, loving the image he gave her.

"You're a greedy little bitch, aren't you?"

If it was anyone else she'd be offended. This wasn't for her to take offence but to relish every part of Raoul.

"Yes. I want you, Raoul. I need you."

"You'll have me. This weekend you're coming back here. We're going to party and fuck. Stroke your clit. I'm so close. I want to hear you scream my name."

He kept talking as she played with her pussy. She didn't stop until she screamed his name, even as Landon knocked on the door to ask if she was all right. When it was over, she called for him to leave her alone.

Across the line she heard Raoul panting. "I'm just cleaning myself off."

"We just had phone sex."

"It's all the rage for long distance relationships."

She removed her fingers from her legs, wiping her wet fingers on her shorts. "I was thinking about you filming." Even though no one could see her she couldn't help but be a little embarrassed by what was happening.

"Yeah?"

"I'd like to give it a try. Even if it's just once, I'd like to be able to watch us together."

"There's a little sex kitten hidden inside you."

"It's your fault. You're bringing her out, demanding that I pay attention to you." She smiled, resting back against the bed. It had been a nice orgasm but nothing like the pleasure his hands and tongue could create. "What's going on in Vale Valley?"

"One of the club whores tried to drug me so that I'd sleep with her and knock her up."

Zoe sat up in bed.

"Really?"

"Yeah, don't worry, nothing happened. I was suspicious of her before I even took a sip of the coffee. One nasty club bitch has been spreading rumors. We're getting to the bottom of it. The good news, you're going to meet Pike and Mary this weekend."

"That's good news?"

"Yep, she's another old lady. You'll like her. She's got the whole sweet gene that you've got."

Shaking her head, she didn't know what to say.

"Anyway, hate to phone sex you and run but I've got to."

Laughing, she said her goodbyes. After talking with Raoul, she felt better, happier.

She left her bedroom to find Landon shooting balls on the pool table. "A great conversation with Raoul then?" he asked, smirking.

"If I tell Raoul you said that, he'd shoot you."

"Nah, he'd clap me on the back."

She walked into the bathroom, washing her hands. There was no way in hell she was being around Landon with the scent of her pussy still on her fingers. "You won't believe what one of the club whores tried to do to Raoul."

Zoe gave him a rundown of what Raoul said to her.

"Well, shit. Raoul did give me a call to warn me when I was next at the club, but to try and force pregnancy, that's against club rules. Suz is going to pay for that."

"The club will handle it?"

"The club handles all of that kind of shit. I wouldn't put it past them to put the fear of God into all of them." Landon handed her a pool stick. "You want to play now that you've relieved your tension?"

Glaring at him, she took the pool stick, even though she wanted to beat him with it.

Chapter Nine

"What does it matter if I told Baby how I stopped being a club whore? She wanted to get noticed, and I simply told her what happened," Suz said.

They were in the basement of the clubhouse. Raoul stood in the corner while Duke, Crazy, and Pike dealt with Suz. She was sitting on a chair, legs crossed, thinking she was something special. Her hair was pulled back into a tight ponytail, and her face was heavily made up with makeup. The fake tits that Crazy paid for were pressed against the front of her shirt, and they looked unnatural even to Raoul.

The last place he wanted to be was in the basement, but he was Diaz's connection so his presence was needed. He held the file that was supposed to come at the barbeque in a couple of days. With Baby trying to drug him, he'd had no choice but to get it himself. The club had a problem if the women thought getting knocked up would end some kind of role they played. Whatever game Suz was playing it was a dangerous one.

"You never fucking drugged me, bitch. I was aware of it."

Suz smirked. "You were awake all right, but you weren't fucking aware of the hole I put in the condom."

Crazy took a step toward her, but Duke held him back.

"I'm surprised you're here. Where's Strawberry? I doubt you left her alone." Crazy's jaw clenched. "No, you wouldn't have left her alone. I take it the fat bitch in the apartment close to ours took it. You should hit that, Crazy. You were always a strange one. I could see you for a chubby chaser."

Pike cut off her words by pressing his hand over her mouth. "Why are we letting this bitch talk?"

"We're not letting her talk. We're finding out that she's the reason Baby tried to fuck over Raoul's drink. I'll find a fitting punishment for Baby, but I think it's time for Crazy to handle this bitch one final time." Duke waved his hand at the woman, taking a step back.

Crazy moved toward Raoul, taking the folder from him.

"Do you want me to let her talk or shall I keep her mouth closed?" Pike asked.

"Release her."

"You think you can scare me?" The moment Pike took his hand away, Suz started talking. "I'm an old lady. You don't hurt old ladies." She smirked.

The smirk was still in place even as Crazy knelt in front of her.

"You're right. We don't usually kill old ladies, but wait a moment. Duke killed his ex-wife for stepping out of line."

The smirk slowly slipped from her face. Raoul watched as the power between the two changed. Crazy needed this. He needed to get away from Suz and to get Strawberry away from her.

"Now, I've got some interesting news for you." He flipped open the file. "I'm going to file for divorce and you're going to agree."

"I'm not going to divorce you," she said. "I won't do it."

"Then you better enjoy a nice long life in prison." He started to extract each incriminating photograph. "I decided to take an interest in my wife's extracurricular activities. Look at what I found out."

There were so many photos of her with other men, but some of the men were not of legal age. One of the boys was in fact sixteen.

Duke had a teenage son and would hate for someone like Suz to have her way with him.

"I was fucking set up. I wasn't told their age."

"I don't give a fuck," Crazy snapped the folder closed. "I've got a shitload of evidence here that will have me rid of you. Now, we've got options."

"What are they?" she asked.

"One, you grant me the divorce and leave here amicably. Strawberry is mine. You don't give a shit about her anyway. I'll have full custody of her." When she went to open her mouth to talk, Crazy held his hand up. "The second option, you fight me, and I expose this shit. I'll fight you every step of the way. The Trojans have done some bad shit but nothing compared to this. You'll be buying your own fucking coffin."

"What's number three?"

All of the brothers tensed as Crazy stood, pulling out his gun, placing it at her temple. "I kill you fucking now and bury your body. I really don't give a fuck which one you choose, Suz. I'd be happier knowing you're fucking dead and not causing another problem for me to fix."

"Strawberry's my little baby."

Crazy shook his head. "No, Strawberry is *my* baby, and your meal ticket. Leanna, our babysitter, is more of a mother to her."

"She's not got what it takes to be me."

"I don't want you, Suz. I never did. You were merely a hole I used to take the edge off." He shrugged. "Leanna's not a whore, or a slut. She's a woman with a warm fucking heart. She's nothing like you."

Raoul watched as she stared around the whole room. "You're going to let him kill me?"

Duke laughed. "I couldn't stop him. I did kill my ex-wife, as I'm sure you're aware of. Think carefully.

You cross us, Suz, and you'll regret it. We don't make a habit of killing women, but we don't exactly not do it either. I'd kill you happily and still go home to my warm bed."

"Then I guess I'll divorce you and keep my mouth shut. You're right, I don't want Strawberry. She's a fucking noose around my neck."

Crazy laughed. "That's okay. She'll never know you as her mother. No kid should know you as its mother."

Raoul left the commotion of the basement while Crazy finished up with his wife.

"I take it my information has been put to good use," Diaz said.

"The best." Raoul shook hands with his friend before slapping him on the back. "You always come through for us."

"I take a nice lump sum out as well, Raoul. I don't go away empty handed." Diaz smiled. "So tell me about your little piece then."

"Little piece?"

"Yeah, Zoe. What's she like?"

"How do you know about Zoe?"

"This is me. I know everything." He slapped his chest, laughing. "Like I know that Lash has taken over the running of The Skulls."

"Wait, what?" Raoul asked, holding his hand up. "Lash has taken over from Tiny?"

"Didn't you know?" Duke asked, coming out of the basement. "It has been a couple of months since he took over. He wants to sit down and have a meet with the Chaos Bleeds crew and the Trojans MC."

"What about the Dirty Fuckers MC? They're ready for a sit down as well. Once a new Prez takes over, there's always a sit down," Diaz said. "I've already had a meet with him. He'll be a good Prez."

"Tiny's still around. He's not left the club, and I imagine he'll be guiding Lash, just like Russ has helped to guide me."

"Guide, my ass. I've done no such thing," Russ said, speaking up from behind his paper.

Raoul laughed. This was what he loved about the club. They were all close and protected each other.

"So, when are you going to do another run?" Diaz asked. "I've got the Mexicans wanting to shift some product."

"I told you. I've got shit to do right now. I'm sure you've got more than enough people to shift the coke."

"No one messes with you, brother. You're untouchable."

Shaking his head, Raoul left the clubhouse to find Mary outside reading a book. She tucked some hair behind her ear, not watching anyone or anything. The club whores were banded together around the side of the clubhouse, smoking a joint. They needed to relax. Baby's future hung in the balance, and if Duke decided he'd kill her, they'd all be terrified.

"What are you reading?"

"A dirty book." She lifted up the cover that featured two men and a woman.

"Okay, wow, you really read this shit?"

"It's not shit. It's educational."

"I feel sorry for Pike."

"When do I get to meet your woman? I heard you're bringing her to the barbeque this weekend."

"I am."

"Are you going to make her your old lady?" Mary asked, looking at him.

"Yeah. I plan to make her mine this weekend. I was going to wait, but I can't."

Pike stepped out of the clubhouse, heading toward them.

"So you're going to have a little Pike?"

"Or a little Mary. I hope I have a little Mary just so he has to work that little bit harder." She smiled, but he saw the love shining in her eyes for the man who'd once hurt her.

"Is everything sorted?" she asked.

Pike stepped behind her, gripping her shoulders while also kissing her head. "What are you reading?"

She opened the book up, and Raoul was surprised to see Pike reading a couple of paragraphs.

"We'll try that tonight."

Mary smiled up at him, jumping down from the wall. "I want to go and visit Holly. She's madder than hell that the doctor has advised her to rest, and Duke's forcing her to."

"I'll be there in a moment. Go ahead and start the truck up."

Raoul watched her leave. She wasn't showing yet with her pregnancy. "You let her read porn?"

"It's not porn, or so she tells me. Besides, that stuff is filled with ideas. You'll soon realize that a way to a woman's heart is finding out exactly what she likes, and sharing it with her. If you love this Zoe, find her weakness and use it to your advantage."

Pike shook hands with him before heading out.

Two of the men had settled down in the club, and Raoul was soon to be the third. Crazy walked out of the clubhouse whistling. He'd not seen Crazy so laid back before.

"What's going on?" Raoul asked.

"I'm getting my divorce. Suz is going to keep her mouth shut, and I can find a more suitable mother for my kid."

"Don't you think that's a little harsh?" Raoul asked. He didn't know a woman who'd be happy with being picked because of her mothering credentials.

"I don't intend for Leanna to find out what I've got planned."

Crazy didn't stay to chat. He straddled his bike, riding out of the clubhouse without a care in the world.
****

"You're coming with us?" Zoe asked, looking at Landon who was putting on a leather jacket.

"Of course he's coming with us. It's a proper barbeque for all the prospects to be present." Raoul slapped his back. "The next couple of years of his life are going to be the best and worst of his life."

"Yeah?" Zoe asked, folding her arms across her chest.

"Yep. He'll have all the pussy he can handle. Shit, they'll be begging for this fucker. His reputation precedes him."

"I really don't need to hear another word about Landon and the bedroom. I think I've heard enough."

She tried her best not to smile.

Zoe and Landon had come to a sort of friendship. He talked crap about sex and girls, she insulted him, and then they played pool where she whooped his ass.

"Anyway, tonight's the night of the barbeque, and we're going to party like there's no tomorrow. Holly and Duke will be there. You'll meet Mary and Pike." Raoul gripped the back of her neck, slamming his lips down on hers. The phone sex hadn't been nearly as good as his lips on hers.

Wrapping her arms around his neck, she pulled him in close, breathing in his musky scent.

"Are you ready to party?" Raoul asked.

When she pulled away she noticed that Landon had gone. "Where did he go?"

"He went on ahead of us. He's only needed around when I'm not here." His hands moved down to cup her ass. "I've missed you."

"And I've missed you."

"Get a skirt to change into."

"Why?"

"I want you to be protected when we're riding my bike, but I want to get to you with ease tonight. I'm going to make you my old lady."

"I thought it was too soon to take me as your old lady?" She was thrilled that he was prepared to make that kind of claim over her.

"No, it's not too soon. I was going to wait, but I don't want to wait anymore." He rubbed his cock against her stomach. "I want to own every inch of you."

She smiled. "Okay. I'll go and get that skirt."

Zoe left him alone, grabbing the best skirt she could find. Raoul was standing by the door with a serious expression on his face.

"What's the matter?"

"There's—" He looked like he wanted to say something else, but instead he shook his head. "Never mind. It's not really important."

"Are you sure? I don't mind sitting and talking if that's what you want to do." She tucked some hair behind her ear.

"It's nothing."

"If you're having second thoughts about tonight I can stay here."

"I'm not having second thoughts. I want to make you my old lady. It's the one thing I'm sure of."

He held his hand out, and she took it without hesitation. She locked up the apartment, following him down to his bike. There was something off about him, but she didn't have a clue what it was. She decided to ignore it. If Raoul wanted to share something with her then she was more than happy to hear it.

Straddling the back of his bike, she placed the helmet on her head, wrapping her arms around his waist.

"One day you're going to let me drive without wearing a helmet."

"Until that day, you're staying safe and wearing a helmet."

She would have blown a raspberry if she wasn't wearing a helmet. Snuggling up against his back, she enjoyed the drive, basking in having him between her thighs once more. One of the highlights of her life was these moments with Raoul. She felt closer to him than anyone else.

The ride was long yet not long enough. She didn't want to let him go. The moment they drove into the clubhouse parking lot, she saw the barbeque was already in full swing. Daisy was at the pit, flipping burgers. The guy she recognized as Russ held a woman his age by his side as he was smearing some kind of grease onto meat.

"Who's Russ with?" Zoe asked.

"Sheila, his old lady. They come around to more of these events now." Raoul didn't add anymore. He took her straight into the clubhouse and up to his room. "Change into your skirt."

"You're very bossy." She didn't bother trying to hide her body from him. Dropping her jeans, she stepped out of them, after kicking her sneakers aside. Pulling up the skirt, she heard Raoul hiss. The skirt was a black one but molded to her hips and ass like a second skin. She'd bought it hoping that it would complement her figure, not show off that she needed to lose a few pounds. Zoe loved eating and wasn't about to stop now just because of Raoul.

"You look fucking hot."

She tugged on her sneakers, pushing her hair off her face, she stood before him. "Am I decent for a barbeque?"

"You're more than decent. I want to mess you up a little and make you completely not decent."

Zoe laughed. "You've always got sex on the brain."

"I can't think of anything better to spend my time than between your thighs."

"You're bad. Anyone ever tell you that?"

"A couple of times. I stopped listening."

He tugged her close, squeezing her ass.

"What will happen tonight?" she asked, nervous about becoming his old lady.

"Some of the guys will go home. The few families that have turned out to party will be gone. I'll take you inside, and someone will watch the door. We won't be disturbed. I'll make you mine inside where the brothers will see but not touch. You'll become mine."

"Don't you think it's a little strange a tradition?"

"No. It works for all the women and all the men. We've never had a problem with the men taking what wasn't theirs to take. Being my old lady, Zoe, it means you support the club. No matter what happens, you can't talk to the cops or anyone else about the club. You can talk to Landon, and any of the other women. No one else."

"Okay. Top secret MC business. I get it."

"Good. Duke won't allow anyone to betray the club."

"I won't."

He cupped her cheek, and she did her best to smile even though she was terrified. The clubs were a different walk of life, one she wasn't used to.

"When you've finished college, I'm going to marry you."

Zoe gasped, laughing, then stopped. "Was that your idea of a proposal?"

"No. You becoming my old lady is a proposal. Marrying you is just so the law knows who you belong to." He grabbed her hand, and she watched in amazement as he slid a ring onto her finger. "As far as anyone's concerned, you belong to me."

"You're a very possessive guy, aren't you?"

"Baby, I've never been possessive in my life, until you."

Zoe stared at the ring, twirling the single diamond around her finger. "Speaking of Baby, what happened to her?" She hadn't wanted to bring it up until she saw him.

"She's out of the club for good. We don't want anyone who is prepared to trick the brothers into getting her pregnant. The other women have been warned. If they try to break our rules, there will be consequences."

"Wow, that bad."

"We don't abide liars or women who try to play their own games. They came into the club knowing what was required of them."

"They can't have a change of heart?"

Raoul locked up his room, shaking his head.

"No, they can't. They had a choice when they first come to the club. That's not going to change."

Zoe shrugged. "It's not my problem. I'm sorry you almost got drugged." She kissed his neck, going on her toes to reach his flesh.

He banded a hand around her. "It's okay. Come on, let's go out and party."

They entered the clubhouse compound, and she saw Holly was standing with her father, and another woman who she didn't recognize.

"That's Mary. She's lovely providing you don't piss her off."

"Do you have firsthand experience with that?"

Raoul closed off once again, and she couldn't help but wonder what she was saying to shut him down. She didn't get a chance to question him as they were pulled into hugs. Several of the men hugged her, smiling, and talking with Raoul. The welcome was amazing and not one she ever expected to get. Raoul wouldn't let her leave his side. A burger was thrust into her hands, and he encouraged her to eat.

When Holly and Mary beckoned her, Raoul shook his head, nodding toward the two women.

Zoe didn't think much of it. It was her first night in the MC. Maybe he was worried that she'd do something to embarrass him.

Landon nudged her with his shoulder. "How are you doing, nerd?" he asked. His arm was around one of the women she recognized, Lori, she believed her name was.

"I see you're going to play when you get the chance."

"Hey, I'm trying to be nice to my roommate. She's sensitive when I take women around to fuck."

"She should be. You're a dirty bastard," Zoe said.

Raoul kissed her head, laughing along with Landon. "Don't mind him. He doesn't know how to keep it in his pants."

"I'm very much aware of what he can't do. The man's a walking advert for diseases or a condom."

All the men laughed at that.

"Baby, you haven't seen nothing yet."

She shivered as Raoul ran his tongue over her pulse, reminding her exactly what they were about to get up to. Zoe couldn't wait.

Chapter Ten

Later that night, Raoul played pool with Landon, Daisy, and Zoe. Several of the guys found their way inside the clubhouse. The tension mounted, and he noticed that Zoe kept rubbing up against his body. Her nipples pressed against the front of her shirt. When she bent over the table to take a shot, he slapped the pool stick against Landon's chest when he caught the guy staring.

All Zoe did was chuckle. "You got a problem with him looking?"

"I've got a problem with him looking when it's mine that he's looking at," he said. She moved in front of him so there was just a small gap between their bodies.

"I'm not yours yet."

Raoul threw the pool stick on the table, calling an end to the game. Sinking his fingers into her hair, he tugged hard on the length. Zoe melted against his body, moaning.

"You were mine the moment I first saw you."

There was a flash of fear in her eyes as she recalled that first time they'd seen each other.

"No, you don't have to be afraid again. I took care of it. I'll always take care of you, baby." He rubbed his face against hers, inhaling her vanilla scent. "They're gone, and they're never going to hurt you again."

"Raoul," she said, whispering his name.

"What, baby?"

"I think I'm in love with you." He pulled away enough to look into her eyes. The fear was back, but this time it was a different kind of fear. This fear was of the unknown. "I didn't mean to—"

He cut off her words with his lips. Sliding his tongue into her mouth, he lifted her onto the pool table.

When he opened his eyes he saw Landon had moved the balls and pool stick out of the way. He was unhindered in his taking of Zoe.

"If I didn't love you, Zoe, I wouldn't be here now. We only take the woman we love as an old lady. I've only known of one case where the guy didn't love her."

"Crazy?"

"Yes. That was different. I'm here because I want to be, and so are you." He opened up the buttons on her jacket, pushing it off her shoulders. Silence had fallen into the clubhouse. He'd been part of several claimings. This was his one and only time he'd ever take an old lady.

Glancing past her shoulder he saw Duke and Pike sitting with their women. Landon had disappeared after taking the balls and stick. Daisy sat at the bar with Pie, Smash, Knuckles, and Chip around the room. Several of the brothers were behind him. He didn't mind their eyes. Raoul hadn't ever had a problem with being watched.

Their gazes were not filled with lust for him or Zoe. They were filled with the promise to protect this woman in front of him. After tonight no other brother would try to take her, but they'd all try to protect her.

She made to push his leather jacket off, but Raoul stopped her.

"No, the leather stays on," he said.

"The rules?"

"Yes, it's my rule." He pulled her in close, taking her lips in a searing kiss. She moaned, gripping his shoulders tightly. The leather protected him from her sharp nails. He didn't doubt she'd leave marks on his body by the end of the night.

"Please, Raoul. I need you." She opened her thighs wider, and he stepped within them.

"You know what's going to happen."

"I know, and I don't care." She went straight for his belt. "If I can't take your jacket off, I can take your pants down instead." She smiled at him. "I'm doing this for you. I want to be with you, no one else. If this is what I need to do to become yours, then I'm more than happy to go through with it."

"You're amazing." He really didn't have any other words to describe how this woman left him feeling. "I love you, baby." Raoul didn't care that the entire room of brothers heard that he loved Zoe. They all knew the truth as he was holding her close to him now. He'd not touched any other woman since Zoe had stepped back into his life.

Tell her the truth.

He couldn't do it. Not here and not now. She'd walk out of his life, and he couldn't bear it.

Tugging her shirt over her head, he flicked the catch of her bra, exposing her tits. He pulled her close against him, wrapping her hair around his fist. Staring into her eyes, he ignored the stares that followed them.

"Ignore them," he said when Zoe looked past his shoulder. "I'm the only one who matters. Touch me, focus on me."

She sank her fingers into his hair, gasping out as he slid his free hand beneath her skirt. He tugged on the thin material of her thong, tearing it away from her body. She jerked at his harsh movements but didn't stop him.

"Grab the condom from my jeans."

Zoe reached into his back pocket taking out the condom he'd placed for this moment. When he got to his room with her, she wasn't going to get the chance to get away from him.

He intended to spend another weekend's worth of fucking her, preparing her ass for him to fuck.

"Please, Raoul."

"I'm going to hold you in place. Take my dick out and slide the latex over me." He held her captive unable to move. This was what he loved about Zoe, along with everything else: she was more than prepared to give the power over to him. He didn't have to fight her to get what he wanted. She gave herself to him willingly.

She tore into the foil packet, and within seconds he was covered with the condom. He had to wait another week before the pill took effect. Raoul wasn't prepared to get her pregnant just yet. He wanted her to finish college before they even considered a family.

"Move to the edge of the table."

Zoe shuffled until she was on the edge.

"Lie back."

She lowered herself to the table. He released her hair long enough to grip his cock, sliding deep within the tight walls of her pussy. Raoul sank his finger into her hair, holding on tightly as rode her pussy hard.

The room filled with eyes disappeared, and Zoe became his only focus. She was so utterly beautiful, open, and breathtaking. He didn't know what he'd done in life to get so lucky to have a woman like her.

Zoe slid her hand between them, stroking her clit as he rode her hard, going deep within her.

"I love you, Zoe. I love you so damn much."

It had been too long since he last was in her pussy. Within minutes he came inside her as Zoe cried out her own orgasm, squeezing his dick in the process. Pressing kisses to her breasts, he lifted her up in his arms. She wrapped her legs around his waist, and he glanced over to Duke.

"It's done. She's protected, and you now have an old lady you need to protect, Raoul." The rest of the brothers nodded in agreement. He'd met the terms, and now Zoe was his old lady.

With his cock still deep inside her pussy, he picked her up and carried her upstairs toward his room.

"Raoul, you're going to hurt something."

"I'm not going to hurt anything. You're my woman, and I'm not leaving your pussy until I have you upstairs." The brothers had seen enough of Zoe's pale skin. They were not going to see more.

"You're going to kill us at this rate."

He handed her the key to open the door. Raoul kicked his door closed, throwing her to the bed. He removed the condom, following her down on the bed.

In quick movements they were both naked, touching each other. "These long distance phone calls are not enough," Zoe said, pressing a hand to his stomach before sliding down to his cock.

Raoul was getting hard once again from her touch.

Leaning over her, he pulled out his cell phone. This was his spare cell phone that he kept in his room.

"How about we make that film? We can watch it whenever we need each other."

Zoe took the phone from his hands. "Okay, but we've got to share this. I don't want a movie that only has my ass and pussy."

"I'd have your tits."

He listened to her pressing buttons. "No, we're not just going to have my tits and my body. I want you. Smile for me, Raoul."

"What do you want, baby?" he asked, lying back.

"None of that fake porn shit. I've seen it online. If I want to get off without thinking of you, I'd watch that." She pointed the phone at his face then slowly slid down his body, resting on his cock. He gripped his shaft, and started to swell.

Zoe bit her lip, her cheeks becoming incredibly flushed as he played with himself.

"Do you like what you see?" he asked.

"Yes."

He took the phone from her, pushing her back onto the bed. She lifted her hands above her head, and he did exactly the same to her. Zoe smiled at him as he pushed her thighs open. He moved the phone close to her core. "You're already soaking wet."

"You're bad."

"But you love it about me."

"I do." She tugged him down, and the rest of the night they took it in turns to use the phone to make their own film.

****

The weeks after becoming Raoul's old lady were a blur. Zoe got caught up with finals at college, preparing for another semester after summer vacation. Her time was spent between college and Vale Valley. She loved spending time with Raoul at the club. When he couldn't make it to her, they would both use the sex video they made together, talking while they watched it. She loved watching that movie and sometimes watched it without masturbating. Zoe loved to watch Raoul. The lust shining in his eyes, the strength of his body, it all helped her to feel safe, especially in the dead of night when she was alone. Holly had the baby a week ago, a baby boy who she'd named Drake. Duke and Drake, not very odd names, but still, she hoped Matthew didn't have an issue with the name. Mary wasn't due with her baby for another couple of months.

Zoe had also been left alone when he went with several Trojans to go meet the new Prez of The Skulls. He didn't talk about what happened there, and so she figured he didn't want to share it.

135

Landon collapsed onto the sofa after they both returned from their final exam.

"Fuck me, I'm pleased that's over for a couple of weeks," Landon said, stretching.

Zoe joined him, closing her eyes as she rested her head against the sofa. "I could sleep for a week."

They'd both been crash studying, neither of them leaving the apartment and using each other to learn.

"I think words are singed behind my eyeballs," Zoe said. "It's all just going to be forgotten."

"When's Raoul coming for you?"

"I don't know. He's not said yet." She rubbed at her temples while her head pounded.

Landon pulled out his cell phone. "He wants me to drive you to the clubhouse."

Zoe groaned. "I'm not up to driving."

"Well, he might have a special party for us. You never know. It's Raoul."

"Let me grab my bag." She climbed off the sofa, padding toward her bedroom. Zoe kept a bag prepared for when Raoul picked her up as a surprise. Flinging it over her shoulder, she saw Landon move out of his room to do the same. "We're becoming like brother and sister."

"Whatever. Please, remind me again why I went to college. I can fuck all night long and never be this tired."

"I've not got a clue why you went to college. I can't even think of a good reason as to why I did."

They locked up their apartment, going for Landon's car. She threw her bag into the trunk, heading into the passenger side.

"So, when do you get to prospect?" she asked, once Landon started the car.

"I don't know. I think after I finish college in another two years. I'm not sure. I was going to talk to

Duke about prospecting now. I don't want to be waiting around to become a member of the club." Landon tapped his fingers onto the steering wheel.

Zoe grabbed her sunglasses, staring out of the window. She was so tired, but her body came to life at the thought of seeing Raoul. He always had this power with her body. It didn't matter what he did, she wanted him more than anything.

Landon turned on some music, and she sang along. They were both still singing as they pulled into the clubhouse. The sun was beaming down, and a lot of the crew turned to look at them.

"I don't see Raoul," she said.

"He'll be here when he can."

Climbing out of the car, she walked toward Holly and Mary. Matthew was sitting at the table, making notes in a book while Holly held her son in her arms. Mary was leaning back on a sun lounger with her hands on her swollen stomach.

"I'm a beached whale. If was I on a beach right now they'd throw me back in," Mary said, moaning.

Zoe laughed, taking a seat beside Holly.

"Hey, you," Holly said.

"How's everyone?" Zoe touched Drake's fingers, loving the way his little hand squeezed hers. "You're going to be so strong."

"How were finals?" Holly asked. Landon had walked over to join them.

"Fucking hard work, that's what." He stretched his neck out. "What are you working on?"

He pointed at Matthew.

"Math. I flunked, and as punishment for not asking for help, I've got to spend the summer brushing up on my skills while all my friends are out partying."

"Your friends didn't flunk math, you did. If they flunked math they'd be forced to stay in all summer," Holly said, moving Drake to her other knee. "Were they hard?"

"Yeah, I don't even want to look at another book again."

Pike walked out of the clubhouse. He knelt beside his wife, kissing her lips before going to her stomach.

"How are you both doing?"

"I'm fine. Baby is fine."

The love shining between the two made her ache for Raoul.

"Where's Raoul?" she asked, surprised he wasn't here by now.

"He's just running an errand for Mac. He owns the diner, and I asked him to do me that one favor. I reminded him that I didn't beat the shit out of him when he deserved it," Mary said.

"You beat the shit out of his bike, Mary," Holly said.

"Look, it was the least I could do. What he did to you prom night wasn't something that should be handled with a slap on the wrist."

"Now who's suffering with hormones?" Pike asked, stroking his wife's arm.

Zoe looked from one person to the other, confused. "What did Raoul do on prom night?"

Holly shut down, but Mary hadn't seen the looks going her way whereas Zoe had.

"Holly didn't have a date when it was prom night. Raoul took her, and her virginity, prom night. He almost lost his club membership for what he did."

Zoe felt like she'd been kicked in the gut. "He took your virginity?"

"Yes, it's all water under the bridge as they say. I'm in love with Duke and wouldn't ever have loved Raoul."

"Zoe, are you okay? You've gone really pale." Landon spoke up.

"I've just come over feeling a little sick." She stood up, and Landon placed a hand under her arm.

"Do you want to go up to Raoul's room until he gets back?" Mary asked.

"No, I don't think I'm up to a visit. If I've got a sickness bug, I don't want to pass it along to your little one." She moved back toward the car. "I know I'm asking a lot, Landon. Will you take me home?"

Raoul had lied to her. He'd lied and made her think she was something special and he'd lied to her. Why would he lie to her?

Climbing into the passenger side, she watched Landon get back behind the wheel. She gave the gang a quick wave, waiting for Landon to pull out of the parking lot.

"I think we should wait for Raoul. Something has obviously upset you."

"I don't want to be here when he's here, Landon. I want to be gone, and if you don't drive, I'll drive myself. Either way, I'm not staying here. I refuse to be here." Zoe turned away from him.

He started the car, peeling out of the clubhouse.

"I'm not comfortable doing this."

Zoe leaned forward putting her head between her thighs. She was hurt, betrayed, angry, and it was all because of Raoul.

You were the one who pursued him.

Damn, why could she have thought for a moment that she'd really mean anything to him?

"Zoe, what's going on?"

"What's going on? Raoul lied to me." She turned back to face the only friend she had. "He told me I was the first virgin he'd ever been with. He never once mentioned to me that he'd fucked Holly or taken her virginity. What is he, the virginity police?" She slapped her palm against the dashboard, angry with her own naivety.

"This is something you really need to talk about with him, not me."

"Why would he? He lied to me, Landon."

"There's a reason for everything. Give him a chance."

She shook her head. "Just take me home. I need time to think." She turned the music on high so that she didn't have to listen to another word that Landon had to say. She was hurting all over. In the last few months she'd shared so much with Raoul. Was it all a lie? No, it couldn't all be a lie. She refused to believe that he'd used her.

He could have.

Zoe had been so easy. All Raoul had to do was snap his fingers for her to go running to him.

****

Crazy sat in Leanna's living room as she put Strawberry to sleep. Suz was out of his life, and he was doing his best to become part of Leanna's world. She didn't give him the time of day, unless Strawberry was involved.

"She's asleep. Are you sure you don't want me to carry her back to your apartment?"

"No. I think she likes sleeping here."

Leanna nodded, picking up the few toys that were lying around. Her space was nicely kept, well cleaned, and childproof.

"When will Suz be by to pick her up?"

"She won't be. I thought you'd have heard. I'm divorcing Suz. She was cheating on me with a lot of other men. I couldn't have that kind of woman around my kid anymore."

"Wow, I'm so sorry. I don't listen to gossip."

She took a seat, giving him sympathetic eyes. He didn't want her sympathetic eyes. He wanted her looking at him with lust or desire.

"No, gossip rarely offers the truth. To be honest, Suz and I, we were only together for Strawberry." He reached over, placing a hand on top of hers. She jumped back, jerking out of his touch. Crazy cursed. She was like a small bird, flying off at a mere touch.

"You've got a beautiful daughter. I can understand wanting the best for her. If you need any help, I'll be more than happy to be there for you." She grabbed their cups from the coffee table. The corners had little white patches of foam that helped with the childproofing. This woman had childproofed her home for him. He really couldn't believe it.

She moved away, going into her small kitchen. He couldn't let her get away. Standing up, he followed her into the kitchen. He wasn't wearing his leather jacket, and with the heat he wore a short sleeved shirt, showing off his muscles. Crazy knew how to capture a woman's attention.

"Can I help you?" he asked, leaning against the doorframe.

Leanna looked over her shoulder, shaking her head. "No, I don't need any help. Do you want another coffee before you go?"

"You want me to leave?" He stepped into the kitchen, moving up behind her. When he placed his hands on either side of her at the sink, he breathed in the strawberry scent of her hair. He loved strawberries.

"What are you doing?" She pulled her hands out of the water, pressing her palm to his chest.

"This." Sinking his hands into her hair, he claimed her lips, sucking her bottom lip into his mouth, moaning as she opened a little and he slid his tongue inside her mouth.

As quickly as the kiss started, she jerked away, shaking her head. "No, I'm not taking over from Suz."

"I don't know what you're talking about." Shame filled him.

"Look at me, Crazy. I know the kind of women you like. I'm not them. You've seen me with Strawberry, and now you're trying to get me take her place. I won't do it. I love your daughter, but I won't be used to become part of her life." Leanna wouldn't look him in the eye. "Please leave my apartment."

"Leanna?"

"No, I'll take care of Strawberry for you. I won't become her mother or whatever you want to use me for."

Crazy stared at her. Tears filled her eyes, and for the first time in his life, he felt torn. He wanted to go and comfort her, but instead of going toward her, he headed to the door. "I'll be back later for my daughter."

She nodded, closing the door behind him.

He had well and truly fucked that up.

Chapter Eleven

Raoul slammed his fist against his old lady's door. He was pissed off, tired, and so angry. When he'd gotten to the clubhouse to have Pike, Mary, and Holly give him the rundown of what happened, he'd wanted to hurt something.

"It's not our fault you didn't tell her, asshole," Mary said.

"Why did you keep it a secret? It's not like it wasn't known. You made sure the whole club knew." This came from Holly.

"Zoe had been a virgin. I didn't want to spoil our time together. I told her she was my first."

A look of understanding had come over the small group.

It didn't matter how much they understood. He was still going to have to fight for Zoe.

Landon opened the apartment. Raoul shoved his way inside and paused when he caught sight of Zoe. She held a pool stick in her hand, and she was glaring at him.

"What do you want?" she asked.

"I wanted to talk to you, baby."

"Baby? You want to talk to me? I thought you'd just find another excuse to lie to me."

Landon brushed past him, picking up his pool stick.

"You can leave," Raoul said.

"This is my fucking apartment. He stays," Zoe said, snapping a ball into the hole. She stared at him, and Raoul almost recoiled from the pain staring back at him.

"I'm sorry."

"What are you sorry about, Raoul? Lying? Getting caught? Not telling me the truth sooner?"

"All of it. I always intended to tell you the truth. I wasn't going to keep lying."

She slammed the pool stick down on the table. He dodged the ball that she threw at him. "You didn't have to fucking lie."

Another ball threw past his head, smashing into the wall. Landon stepped out of the way.

"When you asked me, I didn't want you to think it wasn't special."

"I asked you if I was your first virgin. You could have told me the truth. I wasn't your first virgin. I was your second. Do you love Holly?"

"No, I don't. I've never loved her."

"Then what was it? If you didn't want to tell me the truth what was it with Holly?"

Running fingers through his hair, Raoul felt himself losing her. She was staring at him with fire blazing in her eyes.

"I never cared what Holly gave me. I was a fucking prick, a piece of shit to her. I fucked her, and went back to the clubhouse. I bragged about banging the Prez's daughter." He heard her gasp. "I wasn't a good man. You think Landon's a prick? He's got nothing on me. I got the shit beat out of me by Russ and half the club. I worked so fucking hard to get where I was. I almost lost the club that I loved more than anything. Until a couple of months ago, Holly couldn't even stand to be near me. She hated me, and I deserved it."

"What was I? Did you brag about me? The naive girl you saved."

"No, it wasn't like that. I was in love with you, Zoe. Taking your virginity, it wasn't about bragging rights to a chick I banged. It was real. I understood then what Holly had given me and what I couldn't give her back. I didn't want hers. Being your first, and last, man, that meant more to me than anything. I've grown up since I was with Holly."

Zoe shook her head. "I can't do this."

"What do you want me to do?" he asked.

"I don't want you to do anything. I want you to turn around and get the fuck out of my apartment. I don't want you here." She made to turn away from him.

Closing the distance between them, he slammed his lips on hers, claiming her kiss. At first, Zoe melted against him, and he rejoiced in her body against his. It didn't last. She started to push and shove him away.

"Get away from me." She fought him, but he pushed her up against the wall, trapping her wrists above her head.

"Raoul?" Landon said.

"Back the fuck away, Landon. I'm not going to hurt my woman, but you better stay the fuck back." He'd kill any bastard who tried to interfere with him.

"Don't you dare talk to him like that!" Zoe tried to fight her way out of his hold. She wasn't strong enough compared to him.

"Stop fighting me."

"No!" She screamed the word. "You lied to me."

"You're my old lady, Zoe. You gave yourself to me in the eyes of the club. I'm not going to walk away from you or forget about you."

"I don't want to deal with this shit right now. I don't want to look at your lying face again."

"Landon will stay here with you. I don't expect you to forgive me right away. I love you, Zoe. My heart, my everything, it all belongs to you."

Raoul pressed another kiss to her lips, before moving away. She was panting for breath. The tears she'd kept locked away released, spilling down her cheeks. She rushed into her bedroom, slamming the door closed, cutting him out of her life.

He took a deep breath, his gut in knots at what had just happened.

"I don't care what it takes, you keep her safe. If you need anything, you get in touch with me, do you understand?" Raoul asked.

"Stay. She'll listen to you."

"I hurt her hard. Think about it, Landon. She was still a virgin at twenty. Zoe's beautiful, and I lied to her. Take care of her."

Raoul left her apartment, driving straight back to the clubhouse. Daisy, Crazy, and Knuckles were all sitting at the bar when he made his way inside.

"I fucked up," Crazy said, lifting his finger in the air. "Leanna shot me right down. She already figured out that I wanted her for my kid."

Raoul snatched the whiskey out of Crazy's grip, swigging from the bottle. "Fuck off," he said to her. "My woman just realized she wasn't the first virgin I fucked. She won't let me near her."

He took a long swig of whiskey, relishing the burn as the spirit went down his throat. At that moment in time he'd give anything to get rid of the shit going on inside his head. He was breaking apart, and it was all his own fault.

"Shit, man," Daisy said.

"Yeah, she didn't even hear the truth from me. Mary opened her fucking mouth, not that I can blame her. It's my fault in the first place."

"What are you going to do?" Crazy asked.

"Wait it out. Give her time." Raoul took another swig. He was going to get shit-faced tonight. "What about you?"

"I've got to show Leanna another side to me. Her guard is up now, but I've still got Strawberry on my side. Did you know Leanna smells like strawberries?" Crazy said, his voice slurred. "I'm not going to leave the club tonight. I'd embarrass myself in front of her."

Raoul forced a laugh, checking his cell phone. There were no messages from either Zoe or Landon. He didn't like this.

He'd planned to have a party to celebrate their finals for this year. Instead, he was sitting here, nursing a bottle of whiskey.

Later that night, he took the whiskey to his room, and watched the video of Zoe that was on his phone. He'd fucked up big time, and now all he had as a reminder was this one video on his phone.

No, he wouldn't give up on Zoe. He loved her. She was his old lady. The love of his life. She wasn't going to get away from him that easily.

****

Three days after forcing Raoul out of her apartment, Zoe got a job at a bar in the center of the city. After finding out, Landon had also gotten a job in the same bar. He was pissed to find out she'd taken a job without consulting him.

She knew Landon texted Raoul about her work. The job helped her to stop thinking about Raoul. She'd serve in the bar until the early hours of the morning, dropping down in exhaustion at bed at night. When she woke up, refreshed, Zoe got herself a second job in a café during the day.

Landon was even more pissed off. Her body needed to stop thinking about Raoul. There were times she found herself thinking about him and what had happened. Each time was like a blow to her heart, a physical blow that couldn't be healed with kind words. It was hard to even allow herself to think about him. She wanted him back, and that hurt. Zoe wanted him to suffer like she was. The instant she thought about him, she was tempted to call him.

"If you keep this up you're going to end up in an early grave," Landon said. He'd not been able to get work at the café, but he spent every day sitting here, reading or watching her.

"Is the Trojans worth wasting all of your spare time?" Up until the revelation about Raoul and Holly, she'd believed the Trojans were worth anything to be part of.

You still do.

Get over this.

You love him.

Call him.

Instead of listening to her head, she kept on listening to her heart.

"Yes, they are, and if you weren't determined to not call him, you'd realize they were. Have you spoken to Raoul?" he asked.

She flinched at the mention of his name. This was part of what she hated, that hearing his name spoken aloud caused her to flinch. It was like another element of armor fighting against her. She weakened a little more after hearing his name. "Please don't keep talking about him. I don't want to keep being reminded of him."

"You being his old lady is not going to go away, Zoe. He lied in order to protect you. Yes, I understand why you're hurt, but he loves you. Holly didn't get to be his old lady. You did."

"He lied to save his own ass." She hissed the words at him, wishing he'd keep his voice down. "I don't want to talk about this with you." Zoe ignored his comment about her being his old lady.

You know it's the truth.

You're being stubborn again.

A perfectly good man with a little bit of a past, and you're going to make it difficult for him.

Shut up.

Once she finished her shift at the café, they both went back to the apartment to wash for the bar where they worked. It was more of a dance club than a bar. Zoe pulled her hair above her head, donning the all black uniform the club preferred. They drove together to the bar without talking. She didn't mind the silence as she thought about another year of college, what she'd do afterward. Zoe tried to occupy her thoughts with things other than the man who'd taken possession of her heart and squashed it.

The days turned into weeks, and before she knew what was happening an entire month had come and gone. During that month she'd had a real battle on her hands not to call him. Zoe missed him all the time, and even her dreams were filled of him. During the day she could fight it with the help of exhaustion. Her dreams, however, wouldn't allow her to forget him. She had to constantly fight her own self. College would be starting up again soon. She'd ignored calls from Holly and Mary, and Raoul. He tried to call her, but she just couldn't bring herself to accept his call. Her stubbornness shining through once again. During the night when she heard Landon fucking one of the women he loved to bring back to the apartment, she'd tried to delete the sex tape she and Raoul made together. Her finger had hovered over the delete button, and she'd been unable to cancel it or delete it. She missed him all the time. Zoe didn't even know what the hell she was doing staying away anymore. It seemed a hell of a lot simpler in the beginning. Raoul had lied to her, and she'd run away.

Coward.
You're better than that.
Stubborn.
You want him, you love him, and now you're all alone.
What if he finds someone else who isn't stubborn?

Into her second week of the second month, Zoe was delivering drinks to the tables as they were down a waitress. When she approached one table, she stopped when she caught sight of Duke, Pike, Daisy, and Crazy.

Seeing their leather jackets was like a blow to her system. The very sight of them opened up a whole set of wounds she'd tried to hide from. Raoul's lie had hurt her more than she thought possible. Not only did it open wounds, it awakened her body and all the good memories she'd been trying to run from. Raoul was part of a whole club, a club that had accepted her into his life.

She placed their orders down without looking in their eyes. The moment she went to leave, Duke grabbed her arm.

"No, you don't get to leave. Sit."

"I've got wor—"

"Landon's spoken with your boss. Take a seat. We're not here to hurt you. Believe it or not, you're under our protection."

You love Raoul.
Stop being stubborn.
You're miserable, and only getting older, wasting away.
What are you actually doing this for?
I'm hurting.
Does it hurt as much as being without Raoul?
No.

Over the past couple of weeks, Zoe had found herself weakening, seeing past Raoul's lies, to his true feelings. Holly and Raoul had been in the past, before he'd even met her. It wasn't Raoul's fault that she'd been a virgin, and she couldn't change what he did. He'd become a better man for it.

He lied.

The excuse was starting to wear a little thin, and even she could see she was clutching at something that no longer existed.

Reluctantly, she lowered herself into the nearest seat. "What can I do for you?"

"This shit with Raoul. You've got to forgive him."

"It's not your business, and you shouldn't be com—"

"Raoul is one of my fucking men. I watched him claim you as his old lady. I'm the president of the fucking Trojans. It's my business when someone from my club is hurting. Raoul and you are hurting. This separation is fucking horseshit."

"He lied to me." *Pathetic excuse. You love him. It's in the past. Stop being so bloody stubborn.*

"About you being the only one he took the virginity from."

"How can you even be here now, defending him? It was Holly that he took it from." Her cheeks had to be the color of a strawberry. They were heating every second they spoke to each other.

"No, he didn't take anything that wasn't freely offered. Raoul, Holly, and I have made peace over the shit that happened way before he ever fucking met you. This wasn't months ago, Zoe. This was over three fucking years ago since that happened."

"Why did he hide it from me?" she asked, tears filling her eyes. Duke was doing what she'd been trying to do, breaking her down, opening her eyes. He was fighting her own stubbornness, and making her realize everything she'd been thinking about. "He didn't need to hide it from me." *He didn't want you to not feel special. Raoul made you his old lady. He loves you, and you're being a total bitch to him right now.*

"Really? The first time you found out, you ran. Do you think the news of not being his first would have been any easier?" Pike asked, speaking up. "Our brother is hurting, and he's not focused on the work at hand. In our world, it could get him killed. Do you want that? Do you want him to come home in a body bag?"

She shook her head. "No."

"Do you still love him, Zoe?" Duke asked.

Zoe nodded. "Yes." She'd never stopped loving him, and she hated the fact she'd made them both miserable.

"Then stop this shit. Come home with us. He's hurting more than you can know. What's worse, Zoe? Being the first and never giving a shit, or being the first and it being the best moment of his life? Holly wasn't for Raoul. She's mine, all mine."

"You don't need to tell me."

She nodded, swallowing past the lump in her throat. *Yes, this is what we need. Go to him, you silly bitch.*

"Landon will be driving you. You're not coming back here. Raoul hit the fucking roof when he heard you were working in a bar. He drank himself into oblivion for three days to stop himself coming for you," Duke said.

"Why didn't he come for me?" If at any time in the last month he'd have shown up, she doubted she'd have been able to fight her need for him. She loved him, and she'd been a damn fool.

"He was giving you space," Daisy said. "He loves you."

Landon was already waiting in the car when she left the building. "I'm pleased you've seen sense."

"I'm going to go and talk to him. Nothing else."

"You'll do more than talk when you finally see him."

She didn't say anything else while they drove toward the clubhouse. After the talk she'd had in the bar, the last thing she wanted to hear was how much of a bitch she was being. Zoe had already realized she was being a bitch, and mean, and every bad word she could think about. She had been stubborn, and because of that she'd caused herself over a month of misery. What kind of woman did that?

The drive didn't last as long as she wanted it to. The clubhouse was in full party swing.

"He's in his room," Duke said.

She nodded, not looking at anyone as she made her way towards Raoul's room. When she was standing outside of his room, she raised her hand with her heart pounding. Before she could stop herself, she knocked.

Victory, here is your first step.

"Fuck off."

Okay, he doesn't know it's you. He's thinking it's someone else.

Raoul didn't sound like himself.

She knocked again.

"I said fuck off."

You've been stubborn in keeping him away, so now be stubborn in getting him back.

Zoe didn't give up. She knocked again knowing his temper would make him open the door.

"Are you fucking deaf? I told you to—" The moment he opened the door, Raoul stopped talking.

"What will you do?" she asked, smiling.

153

He looked a mess. His hair was all over the place, and he had to have a month's growth on his face. Raoul looked like he lived on the streets not in the clubhouse. Even under all of his clothes she saw he had lost too much weight. The guilt hit her hard. They had both been miserable because of her stupid behavior. She was a first class bitch, and she had to make it up to him.

"Zoe."

"Raoul."

All of her anger and hurt dissolved at the sight of him. She'd been hurting, but so had he. Without waiting for an invitation, she walked into his arms, slamming the door closed behind her.

"You stink," she said wrinkling her nose. "Really bad."

"I've not found the time to shower."

"Ew, that's totally gross." She kept her arms wrapped around him and walked him through to his bathroom.

"Am I dreaming right now?"

"If you are, lucky you. I'm not dreaming. You stink, really bad. The worst smell in the world."

She released him long enough to run him a bath. Every now and then, he reached out to touch her.

Unable to hold back, she cupped his cheek, staring into his sad eyes. "I forgive you, and even though I don't deserve it, I hope you can find it in your heart to forgive me. I've been a total bitch, so wrong, and so damn stupid. I'm really sorry."

"Thank you so much, baby. There's nothing for me to forgive. You were hurting, and Holly meant nothing to me, Zoe. I mean it. She was just a fucking chick I banged."

Pressing her palm over his mouth, she shook her head. "No, I don't need to hear anything else from you. I don't need to know why you did or what you felt. I'm your old lady, and you love me, right?"

"More than you can know, and yes I forgive you. I can't bear to go on living if you're not in my life. I'm in a bit of a shock right now that you've admitted to being a bitch to me."

Tears filled her eyes. "I'm here, Raoul. I'm not going anywhere, and don't push it."

He took hold of her hand that still bore his wedding band. "You didn't take it off?"

"No, I couldn't bear to take it off. You're still going to marry me?" She bit her lip, hating how sad she sounded even to her own ears.

"Yes, I'm going to marry you."

She finished putting the water into the bathtub. Staring into his eyes, she removed her shirt, followed by her pants and underwear. Climbing into the water, she held her hand out. "Are you coming in?"

Raoul tore his clothes off, climbing in the water behind her. She gave him enough space to wash before she rested against him.

"I've missed this," she said. Zoe stroked his arms where he held her.

"I missed you."

"I missed you as well. I never want to go through that again." She heard him sigh, and seconds later he kissed her head. "Why did you lie to me?"

"I was scared."

"What?" She was so shocked that she jerked around to look him in the eye. "You were scared?"

"What happened with Holly was before I even knew you existed. I never intended to sleep with Holly that night nor take her virginity. I was such a fucking bastard to her. I didn't care."

"I've heard this."

"I didn't tell you because the truth is, I may have taken two women's virginity, but you were the only one I cared about. I didn't want to hurt you. The thought of hurting you even just a little kills me, Zoe. I love you. I love you more than I ever thought possible for a woman."

"I love you, too."

"No, you don't understand. Women were mere fuck holes for me. Then you came along, and everything changed. From that night I couldn't stop thinking about you. You were in my heart long before you showed back up here to see me."

She chuckled, recalling the night that she had just turned up. "You weren't exactly in the best position to be receiving visitors."

"No. It was you I was thinking about. I didn't give a fuck about anyone else. I was thinking about you as I fucked another woman. I'm not proud of what I did with Holly. I can't change it, and if I could, I would."

She pressed her hand to his chest. "Stop apologizing. You don't need to. I've put us both through enough hell to last us a couple of years. I was hurt, and I worked my ass off just to stop myself from remembering you. I should have known it wouldn't work."

"I'm glad it didn't."

Zoe told him about Duke and some of the boys coming to see her.

"They didn't frighten you, did they?"

"No, they opened my eyes and made me realize I was angry and wrong for it."

"You weren't wrong for being angry at me."

"I was for running away like that. I was running from something neither of us could change." She stared up into his beautiful blue eyes. "I won't run again. I promise."

"I won't hold anything back or lie to you either."
He leaned down, kissing her head. "I love you, Zoe."

"And I love you."

She snuggled up against him, happy and content to finally be in his arms. There was nowhere else she'd rather be. The past month she'd been living a lie.

"I'd have come for you soon," Raoul said.

"You would?"

"Yeah, I didn't want to lose my reputation, Zoe. I'm never going to let you go. If you're ever pissed at me again, don't expect me to allow you to be gone for this long again." He kissed her temple, and she chuckled. Slowly, the kiss went from just a gentle touch to something more. He kissed down her neck, sucking on the flesh right above her pulse. His hands moved down from her stomach, going between her thighs.

His fingers slid against her pussy with ease. She was so wet that nothing hindered his touch. He caressed over her clit, and Zoe let herself go in his arms.

Reaching behind her, she wrapped her fingers around his length, giving him pleasure just like he was giving her.

"That's it, baby. When we're out of this bath, I'm going to fuck you so damned hard, you're never going to remember you were away from me for a month."

Zoe moaned, thrusting her pussy onto his fingers. She hadn't experienced any great orgasm in the past month. Her body rebelled against her own fingers.

"You know me, Zoe. This body knows its master."

She whimpered at his touch, knowing he spoke the truth. There was no one else she wanted, no one else she trusted in the world with her body.

The peak of her orgasm was nearing, and from Raoul's heavy breathing, he wasn't going to last much longer.

They came together, calling out each other's names as their release rode them both hard. When it was over, she didn't waste any time. She turned around, not caring that his seed was spilled in the bath. The room was small enough that she was able to reach over him, pressing her breasts against his face. She filled the sink and grabbed a razor. Zoe started working on his facial hair.

"This has to go," she said.

"You don't like my growth?" he asked, running his hands up and down her body.

"No, I don't. It's gross." She loved the way his hands were always on her body, touching her. They were both making up for lost time.

It took her a good twenty minutes, and the water was nearly cold by the time she finished. Cupping his cheek, she ran her thumb along the smooth skin. "All better."

Raoul reached between them to his already erect cock.

"I'm making up for a month of not having your pussy."

Zoe had no complaints. She was on the pill, and she lifted over his cock, sliding down onto his length, taking him to the hilt. He filled her to the point of pain, but again, she no longer cared.

All that mattered was the love she felt for this man, this man who was once a cad but now the love of her life. Zoe held onto him tightly, never wanting to let go.

Raoul whispered words of love against her ear as they fucked in the bath. He gripped her ass with one hand

while the other sank into her hair, holding
tight against his body. It was perfect, and ↲
was never going to stop being like that.

    ****

The following morning, Crazy had a full
migraine as he made his way up to his apartment.
didn't knock on his door though. He went straight for
Leanna.

It was early, and Landon had dropped him off
home. He still had too much liquor in his system to allow
him to drive.

She opened the door, pulling together a silk night-
robe.

"Crazy?"

"Hey, baby."

"It's early." She reared back a little once she got a
whiff of him. "You're drunk."

"I'm not coming for Strawberry. I just wanted to
say something to you."

"Crazy, whatever it is can it wait until you're
sober?"

"No, it can't. I refuse to wait another moment."
He leaned heavily on the door. "You were right. I was
going to use you for Strawberry, but I'm not going to do
that anymore."

"You're drunk. I don't think we should be talking
about—"

"I'm not going to give up. I no longer want you
for my kid, Leanna. I want you for myself, and I will
have you."

Those were his last words before he turned away,
leaving her shocked. He walked into his apartment, and
slept off the drink he'd consumed the night before.

Epilogue

Zoe stormed into the clubhouse angry at the orders she'd just received from Landon that Raoul wanted her now, and if she didn't come, he was going to spank her ass. How dare he order her around? It had been four months since that night they'd made up in the bath, but that didn't mean he could order her around.

In the last four months they had shared everything together, their hopes and dreams, their loves, and of course sex. She couldn't get enough of him, and he couldn't get enough of her.

"Raoul, where the fuck are you?" she asked.

Her pussy was slick from the warning he'd given. He was going to spank her ass? She couldn't wait. They had been experimenting in the bedroom lately, and she liked a little bit of pain mixed in with her pleasure. She also loved it when Raoul fucked her in the ass, which was a total surprise to her. He'd taken his time in preparing her to take his cock, but after that first time, she found herself loving it.

When she rounded the corner of the clubhouse, Zoe froze. The back of the clubhouse had been transformed into a beautiful aisle. Raoul moved toward her, and he'd been standing by the priest when she walked in.

"Raoul, what's going on?"

He didn't speak a word, merely went down on one knee before her. With her heart pounding, she took the hand he offered.

"I think you and I both know what this is, baby." She stared at the clubhouse that was filled with Trojans.

"I'm not sure."

"You're the love of my life, Zoe. You're already my old lady, and it's time I made you my wife." He rubbed his thumb across the ring already decorating her finger. "Will you do me the honor of becoming my wife?"

"Yes, yes, yes." He got to his feet, and she flung herself into his arms. She held him tighter than anything she'd ever held in her life. "I love you, Raoul."

"I love you, too, baby."

"Will I be conducting the ceremony today?" the priest asked.

"You will."

They didn't waste any time. Zoe didn't need a big church wedding or to have hundreds of guests. This was perfect, a wedding at the club, binding herself to Raoul for the rest of her life.

She smiled at Holly and Duke, who held little Drake, with Matthew by their side. On the other pew there was Mary and Pike with their daughter, Starlight. She'd gotten close to the other two women in the last couple of months. They were her friends, and the Trojans were part of her life along with Raoul.

The ceremony lasted minutes, but she didn't look away from Raoul the entire time. This was right. When the priest pronounced them husband and wife, Raoul's lips were on hers, and in that moment she knew an eternity with him would never really be long enough.

She'd take what she could get, and later that night, Raoul showed her with actions and words, how important she was to him.

The End

www.samcrescent.wordpress.com

LUST

Evernight Publishing

www.evernightpublishing.com

Printed in Great Britain
by Amazon.co.uk, Ltd.,
Marston Gate.